ST. EDMUND WOOD

A CHESHIRE TALE

ELLEN L. EKSTROM

WHYTE ROSE & VIOLET, SCRIBES

St. Edmund Wood – A Cheshire Tale
ISBN: 978-0692428450

Published in the United States of America

Cover design: Whyte Rose & Violet Artists

Images courtesy of Adobe Stock and iStockPhoto.com

Whyte Rose & Violet, Scribes

www.whyteroseandviolet.net

queries@whyteroseandviolet.net

In memory of strong women everywhere.

ST. EDMUND WOOD

A CHESHIRE TALE

CHAPTER I

THE STORY INSOFAR as anyone cared began in a rattling, noisy coach from London; a conversation shared by two strangers as different as night and day that started with a look. After stealing surreptitious glances at her traveling companion, The Elderly Woman of Means put aside her copy of Fordyce's Sermons and gazed at The Young Lady through spectacles, nodding.

"*You've* been to London for the season!" The Woman pronounced.

The Young Lady sitting opposite shook her head though it was barely a movement. She resumed her vigil on a rural landscape far more entertaining than this curious woman.

"Can this be so? Who are your parents, my dear? Why would they not consider bringing you out?"

"It wasn't a question of consideration." The voice was soft, quiet, and clear, but not the childish or nasal kind. It was a voice that inferred confidence, even contentment.

"Ah…" Eyes darted up and down. "Well, I see that you have an eye for the latest fashion, for if I'm not mistaken, that dress is very much like the one Mistress Beaulieu wore on the Glorious Twelfth when she joined the Duke of Clarence and his hunting party!"

"Is it? I didn't know."

"Oh yes! The sash is just at the waistline and affords a freedom of movement you modern girls so love—let me hazard a guess. You're not wearing corsets!" The last was said behind the woman's fan. "You do have an uncommon beauty, my dear! Well, it is a shame. Not that your beauty is a shame, nor going without a corset! It is, I meant, a shame your parents did not see fit to bring you out, for it is certain you'd have the pick of suitors from the best houses in society!"

The Young Lady smiled and offered another imperceptible shake of the head.

The coach slowed and began its descent through a wood and into the valley where a village clustered around the walls of a ruined castle. The bleating of the post horn made the woman pause only for a second in her accolades. "We should be approaching Litchfield, I think, for I see the towers of a castle!"

"We're too far north for Litchfield. We must be near Crewe, or perhaps Warrington?"

"Knowstone!" the driver shouted.

"Oh…" A disappointed sigh.

Not that anything more need be said of a village in the middle of nowhere; a forgotten place beside the ruins of a forgotten castle.

The coach made its way up and down the streets of the village, careening and tipping as corners grew tighter and narrower until it groaned and creaked to a halt at the common room door of the only inn for miles around, The Castle and Motte.

The considerable noise and the lantern light woke a gnarled creature asleep on the stoop. It stood more upright than customary, swaying back and forth while a palsied hand groped for something to steady unwilling thirty-year-old legs; here was a commentary on the local economy; here was a man brought to a sorry state by life and liquor. His name was Abraham Creetur, and his nickname was apt: 'The Creature.'

The Creature stared blindly into the carriage lanterns, trying to bat them away as if they were insects. "Here! What're ye doing? Weren't 'pected 'til the morrow!" he growled.

The driver threw down a shilling and waved him off. "Knowstone, Miss!" he then called and rapped hard on the coach roof. A moment later, the door opened, and The Young Lady disembarked, her face obscured by a scarlet hood. She waited as the footman brought her trunk down and pointed toward the public-house door when asked where she wanted it.

The Creature caught sight of her as she approached and stepped back. "You! You came back!" he growled. "Isn't true you be dead! Isn't true at all!" Having said this, The Creature moved away, watching her suspiciously. The coach drove off and then disappeared into the wood, becoming a speck of light on the horizon until it was swallowed up in the trees. The Young Lady glanced down the lane to her left, then to her right, then left again. A tentative scuff of her boot became a step and another, and soon she paced a wide arc as she waited. The church bells rang the half-hour and were ringing seven o'clock when The Creature lost interest in her and settled under his cloak for the night.

"Why don't you go home?" he muttered.

"It's too far to walk with my trunk. I have to go through St. Edmund Wood."

He cackled, adding, "Best not go through St. Edmund Wood at night! Safe for no one—not even you!"

A moment passed before The Young Lady replied. "I can pay you a ha'penny if you'll escort me and bring the trunk. No? A half-crown, then." The offer was conveyed in a voice now unsure and tremulous. The self-assurance of an hour past was gone.

The tantalizing sound of metal jingling at the bottom of a purse and the shine of a new coin held up in the lamplight made him game for only a second. He was ready to accept the offer and his trembling claw of a hand was willing to take it when he paused and shook his head.

"No! I daren't—not worth risking bed and board!"

"And where could you earn a half-crown doing so little, Abraham Creetur?"

"Not fair, Mistress! Not fair!"

"Suit yourself."

The Creature sighed with relief when he heard the chink and rattle of coin against coin and the snap of a purse clutch.

It meant he was free of an obligation. The Young Lady began pacing again, and she stopped before him, meeting his gaze. The Creature looked away first.

"I don't understand. Cook should have been here to meet me…"

The Young Lady might have spoken to the wind, for The Creature was snoring, his breath making clouds above them. She watched in fascination for a moment and then tried the public-house door. Of course it would be unlocked; sunset was but an hour past. She took a breath and went in.

"Christ and all His Saints!"

The Innkeeper heard the door slam and had come out to greet the new customer but stopped just short of the hearth when he saw who it was. The Young Lady had pushed back the hood of her cloak, and the men in the common room turned from conversation and ale to offer appreciative stares. Only A Young Clergyman taking his supper seemed disinterested until he noticed how silent the room had become and looked up. He pushed aside the books and papers that perpetually cluttered his usual table in his usual corner beside the hearth and reached for the bottle of wine, throwing a glance at her.

"Who's she?" The Young Clergyman asked a man nearby.

"A ghost." A cryptic response, that, but The Young Clergyman shrugged, looked about, and frowned, seeing how the men leered and whispered among themselves.

"Why should you come here?" The Innkeeper demanded of her.

The Young Lady took a tentative step forward as if the wooden planks beneath her light step would give way. "Cook was supposed to meet me. I've been waiting for the better part of an hour. I've come for supper."

"Supper was an hour ago, Miss!"

"Please, I've come a long way. Even some bread and butter, a cup of ale."

"Didn't you hear me?" The Innkeeper hissed. "Supper's

done! There's nothing to be had!"

The Young Lady kept her eyes on The Innkeeper. When he didn't budge, she took a booth under the stairs, and there she sat for the longest time, staring down at her hands folded neatly on the filthy tabletop.

"It is your bounden duty to feed the hungry," she spoke up as The Innkeeper brushed past to answer the town magistrates' bellowing for more ale.

"Don't tell me what my duty is!" The Innkeeper growled.

"If I were a clerk from London or a shopkeeper from Chester or Litchfield, or Warrington, you'd not waste a moment arguing. You'd not argue over the color of my coin."

The Innkeeper threw down his towel and spun about, grumbling about the importance of some people. He grabbed a plate of meat and cheese from a table near the door, food that had been sitting out for most of the day, if not picked over by rats or humans. A pitcher was slammed on the tabletop so that it sloshed and spattered the girl's cloak, the plate thrown down with a clatter. A tin cup tossed at her spun like a top until she reached out to steady it.

"It's gone bad," she spoke up after a glance at her supper.

The common room fell quiet. All eyes turned in her direction.

"It's gone *bad*," she said again, this time meeting The Innkeeper's smirk with a sad, serious stare.

"It's all I have at this hour," the innkeeper snapped. "If you wanted supper, you should have come earlier."

"That's no fault of mine, sir. I've no say over the weather or the roads," she replied. Her eyes lighted on The Young Clergyman and nodded in his direction. "Ask the vicar. I'm sure he'd agree."

A Serving Girl passing by shook her head at The Young Clergyman as if to warn. He pretended interest in the Bible open on the table and avoided The Young Lady's large eyes boring into him.

But he did want to know what color those eyes were.

"It's all I have," The Innkeeper spat. "Find supper in London, bloody Chester, or Litchfield if my fare isn't good enough!"

"It is your bounden—"

The kitchen door slammed shut behind him.

Conversation and music rose slowly in the common room until the incident was just another passing entertainment at The Castle and Motte, something to be recounted after church in the morning. The Young Lady was forgotten. She shoved the plate from her and drew the pitcher close. Glancing down into the pitcher to make sure nothing floated on top, she poured a cup and drank, screwing up her face.

The Serving Girl stopped by the table, took from her apron pocket a fresh, warm sweet bun and an apple, and placed them on a clean napkin. No one watched or knew; no one, save The Young Clergyman, the Reverend Mr. Godwin Herrold.

"Bless you for your charity, Dorcas," he murmured when The Serving Girl came his way. She pulled another bun out of her pocket and let it roll onto his plate. "What's her name?" Godwin Herrold whispered, taking a bite, and savored the sweetness, looking at The Young Lady.

Dorcas now leaned in as if to wipe up a puddle of grease and crumbs. "Witherslack."

Godwin pushed his tankard at Dorcas and watched the fresh ale she poured swirl into a frothy head, making note of the name.

Witherslack.

When he left the common room at midnight, The Young Lady was still sitting there, staring at nothing, waiting.

CHAPTER 2

"AN EXCELLENT HOMILY, Mister Herrold! I don't believe we've heard two entirely different scriptures so neatly bound up! The Feeding of the Five Thousand and David and Bathsheba? Profound, sir!"

"I don't see Miss Witherslack," Godwin said aloud to himself, looked about, and ignored the effusive praise of John Merrow, Esquire, the Mayor of Knowstone. He looked over his shoulders at the worshippers as they came out of St. Ælfgiva's Church, ignored their voices gradually rising as they came down the path to the gate, nodded absently to inquiries about his health or the new catechism class starting up, how he was settling in and getting on. Merrow was a small man but large in girth, and he blocked the path for some, the view for Godwin.

"Perhaps you'd like to join us for the hunt next weekend?" Merrow asked.

"I don't hunt," Godwin replied, still looking.

"The devil take me, you say! You seem to be hunting for someone!" Merrow chortled and then laughed at his joke.

"I was looking for Miss Witherslack."

"Miss Witherslack? Mistress, you mean. She's right there, Mister Herrold." Merrow gestured at a woman shaded by a chestnut tree and standing apart from the other church-goers.

"Ah! That must be her mother. I see the resemblance."

"Do you mean Mistress Burnley? She that was Mary Witherslack?"

"Yes, I suppose that's her name. She came into The Castle and Motte last night."

"How could you have known?" Merrow asked. "You won't find her in church, Mister Herrold, and there's the truth of it. Something's not right with her."

"What's this?" John's wife Katherine joined them, smiling prettily at the handsome young cleric.

"Mister Herrold was inquiring of Mary Burnley, dearest," answered Merrow.

"Ah. Mistress Witherslack's daughter. The late Reverend Witherslack's only child and daughter. She's come back to Knowstone, a widow and childless after eighteen months of marriage."

"Then perhaps you will accompany me on a pastoral visit, Mistress Merrow?" Godwin suggested. "To offer comfort and friendship in her time of need. I took by her reception last night she has returned home to few friends."

"It would be a waste of your time!" Katherine pronounced.

"You're a stranger here, Mister Herrold," Merrow spoke up. "You'll find that Mary Burnley only wants to be left alone."

"Left alone!" Katherine spat. "Strange words for it! I'll tell you what others in the village will not—that Mary Burnley is an example to our young unmarried girls of Knowstone. She is what they must not become! She is a lesson to be learned." There was too much emphasis on the word 'she.'

"If we have a Mary Magdalene or a Jezebel in our congregation, then spiritual guidance and comfort are what is needed," Godwin jested. "And our forgiveness," he added pointedly.

"It is worse than that!" Katherine said.

"Indeed?" Godwin queried and prepared to leave. Katherine held him back.

"Do you not think, Mister Herrold, that widows should comport themselves in a dignified manner as befit their station and not be all froth and lightness, to be in love with life?"

"I would I knew what you meant, Katherine Merrow."

He discovered her meaning on market day that week

when he caught sight of Mary Burnley walking through the village with unkind stares and whispers following her.

Her pale blue frock skimmed lightly over the snow-dusted lane as if she were no more than a feather or soap bubble. She was nothing like the big-boned, large-breasted townswomen; she was round where a woman ought to be round, but there was a litheness to her movements, which were graceful and with economy. There was a distinct sensuality to her person that hadn't given way to the thickness that sometimes cursed married women.

Every woman out on market day was wearing her best cap or bonnet, but not Mary Burnley. Her hair was tied up by dark blue ribbons. Locks of chestnut-colored hair escaped as she strolled through the square; they danced and sailed in the breeze, caught the mid-morning sun, and shot copper and amber motes. The January morning was bitterly cold and brought rosy color to her cheeks and lips. Her light-colored, round eyes observed everything and nothing, for she was other-worldly. All these attributes came together in absolute perfection.

The breeze suddenly gusted and took up one of those hair ribbons. It sailed and danced, then dropped at Godwin's feet. She was quicker than Godwin and caught the ribbon in long, beautiful fingers.

"*Oh!*"

With that exclamation, she stood upright, now face to face with Godwin, and pushed back her hair. They smiled at one another—one of those tentative smiles replete with sexual tension and curiosity—until she dipped in a neat curtsey and hurried on her way.

"…it isn't any wonder that her husband died poor!"

Godwin shoved away from the lych-gate when he heard the comment from Katherine Merrow. She and her companion Anna Bigod were coming through the churchyard on their way to the church to polish the brasses and deliver clean linen.

"He was a professor of antiquities or history. I heard he

had no interest in money," Anna sniffed. "Except when it came to spoiling her with a new frock or trinket! Two and five for a pair of lace gloves from Florence! *From Florence!*"

"Well, he might have left her something for a black dress!"

"Good morning, ladies," Godwin greeted. "Who needs black mourning cloth? Perhaps we can find something in the cupboards."

"It wouldn't do any good," Katherine sighed. "Mistress Burnley wouldn't wear it. Now, we'll polish the brasses, and you won't even know we're here, Mister Herrold." Yet, as Godwin sat and wrote letters at the sacristy desk, their conversation intruded on his thoughts, the word 'Mary' catching his attention.

"…she came to the choir practice as if nothing had happened and sang with us, again, as if nothing had happened! All smiles and sweetness, that one!"

"You know, of course, why she doesn't come to church?"

"Not her father—!"

"No, my goodness, no! All that learning in Oxford."

"Surely not she? A student?"

"That I wouldn't know, Katherine. But her husband, the late Mister Burnley, it is said, had a fondness for teaching women to be equals in all things, including education."

"As long as a girl knows her letters and numbers to keep the household accounts and scripture lessons to teach the children, what else is there need of? She can keep her husband by the usual means. You don't need an education for that."

The women giggled here.

"Katherine Merrow, for shame! And I think there is something else: she has set herself up as a tradeswoman! She weaves cloth and sells it. She walks all the way to Chester to trade with the dressmaker and the cathedral. I wouldn't be surprised if this is her linen—Katherine Merrow, look what you've done! I shall have to boil it now to remove the stain! She'll have to come with more linen!"

Godwin went out into the sanctuary and saw the stain of

red wine spreading over the fair linen on the credence table. He held the untainted corner between a thumb and forefinger, feeling the smooth softness of the fibers. The fabric's quality was exquisite, and in that mitered corner, he saw the initials 'M' and 'B' stitched almost invisibly.

"I'm sorry, Mister Herrold! The cruet was over-filled with wine. I'll fetch a new cloth," Katherine apologized as she grabbed for the linen. She threw it down and ran to the sacristy. Godwin knelt to pick it up and noticed how the stain had spread to the corner and looked almost like blood as it covered the initials. Anna stared at him while polishing a candlestick absently and smiled back.

"She's trouble, that one."

Godwin couldn't help but wonder if she meant Katherine Merrow or the mysterious Mrs. Burnley.

That evening as he walked to The Castle and Motte, Godwin remembered bits of conversation and the feel of the linen. While he ate his solitary supper in his usual booth at his usual table in his usual corner by the hearth, with books and papers spread before him, Godwin listened to the hushed conversations of the men of Knowstone. They spoke of corn prices, the foaling of Sir Martin Frankewell's prize Arabians, the price of wool, and how much milk the Galthwaite cows would give. And Mary Burnley.

"Perhaps someone would tell me what it is about Mary Burnley that gives rise to so much interest. I see she is quite beautiful, but aren't there beautiful women in Knowstone? In Cheshire?" Godwin laughed, looking around at the patrons.

The room fell into silence, and heads turned in his direction with amazement on their faces. And then one of the Frankewell servants spoke up.

"*Poor Mistress Witherslack!*"

Chapter 3

Mrs. Emily Witherslack was disconsolate. All the misfortune of the world rested on her weary shoulders, what with the death of her beloved husband two years ago, and now this.

"I don't know what to make of it," she sighed and cast a dramatic look at her guest, The Reverend Mr. Charles Talbot, Vicar for St. Ælfgiva's Church. Talbot shook his head in sympathy.

"And you say he left no income to be disposed of or a legacy?"

"His debts exceeded one hundred pounds! That he should take rooms in a manor at Oxford–and not just any rooms, mind you, but the best rooms in Grafton Manor, and then rooms in London at Carlisle House—Carlisle House, of all places! It is certain we are disgraced. How long will it be before the solicitors come to my door with their writs and petitions, their warrants? I blame her! I would I knew what to do with her!"

"Perhaps his family can be of assistance. Did you not say his father is the rector of Saint Mary's Liverpool?"

"Liverpool! A place as bad as Plymouth or Birmingham!" Emily spat.

Talbot stirred his tea for lack of better entertainment and let his eyes slide from the comfortable parlor of the Witherslack house to its Mistress, Percy Witherslack's attractive widow. She was a handsome woman, but that was his only charitable opinion of her. He preferred women round in form and complaisant, demure and silent—the more consistently silent, the better—everything that recommended a lady of quality in his mind. Everything Emily wasn't. Emily had a high opinion of herself, held an opinion on everything, and was always willing to share it. Her voice was brittle and high-pitched as it happened with women who thought themselves above their peers and station. She was tall and lithe with her Welsh ancestors' dark hair, the large dark eyes of a doe, and a passion for all that was fashionable in good society. She could claim an ancestor to one of the most famous kings, Alfred, and his descendants, one of them from Cheshire. There was nothing soft or feminine about her frame or personality. Strange how such a severe woman with such cold beauty could give birth to one such as Mary Burnley. Were Talbot disposed to choose a wife from among the ladies of Knowstone, she would not be Emily Witherslack.

Talbot had little room or cause to talk. If it were possible that an insect could walk upright and speak, that would describe Charles Talbot. Gangly, impossibly thin, and with frighteningly large eyes that missed nothing (especially the slightest infraction), his judgmental stare made him few friends.

Now he coughed when he noticed Emily's scrutiny and stirred his cup of tea, this time thoughtfully.

"Then perhaps Mister Erland Frankewell?" Talbot suggested.

Emily threw her hands up in despair. "Ah, now there's a deep wound! I'm sure when it got about that my daughter returned, the Frankewells were the first to snigger behind their hands and start the ugly rumors! I shall have to leave Knowstone! I am forever in disgrace! I shall go back to London. There's nothing else! To think that after all these years in Knowstone as the wife of the vicar! I'll live with my sister. She has a large house in Mayfair. She has an income of one hundred and twenty pounds per annum left to her by her late husband, Mister Lodge. She must take pity on my situation, for there is none else!"

"Your situation, Mistress Witherslack?"

"Of course it is my situation! I hear the sniggering and whispers. I see the looks! It is my situation when I am no longer invited to tea or to dine. Not even to the assembly ball! And all because of a willful, disobedient child!"

Talbot removed his pocket watch and studied it, then coughed.

"I have a remedy for that cough, Mister Talbot, should you have need of it." The words came out brittle and cold, biting.

"I wonder if any part of your misery or grief is for the girl."

Now Emily hurled herself out of the chair and paced the length of the room and back. She jabbed a bony finger at him, saying, "She took it upon herself, Mister Talbot! She did not listen to her father or me! All that has befallen her, all that has happened, well, there's a saying that if you make the bed, you lie in it–and we know that's what she wanted, wasn't it? Now see what's happened!"

"I'll leave you now, Mistress Witherslack. The bishop has called a meeting for tomorrow in Chester, and I must prepare. No, no, don't trouble yourself. I'll see my way out. Commend me to Mistress Burnley. Good day."

Emily and Talbot exchanged sterile smiles and nods of their heads in farewell. They were the most despised people in Knowstone, and neither knew it, being consumed by separate yet equal ambition for more than what was given them.

Emily glanced at the mantle clock and knew no one else would come to call; she spent the remainder of the afternoon watching her daughter Mary Burnley work the loom in the far parlor, wondering what would become of the girl, but more importantly, what would become of herself.

Mary ignored her mother's sighs and vituperate glances, concentrating on the fair linen taking form beneath her heddle. The bottoms of crosses started to appear against a smooth, plain ground. She remembered when she first thought of the design, for it came from the cross that hung around Justin's neck. A year ago, she lay in Justin's arms and listening to his heartbeat, feeling the heat of his body on hers. It would be difficult, perhaps the most difficult thing Mary Burnley would ever do, to pretend that the last eighteen months had never happened.

The cadence of the loom as it worked was like a heartbeat, like a voice that calmed Mary and whispered, '*Soon, very soon. Soon, very soon.*'

Justin's voice whispered in her ear.

"*Soon, very soon, my love…*"

The cadence became the gentle swaying of the coach taking them away to London, Mary being lulled closer to sleep as she listened to Justin's heartbeat…

"I shall never be forgiven," Mary whispered sadly.

"You've done nothing that requires absolution, dearest!" Justin murmured into her hair. Just taking in the scent of him calmed Mary's frayed nerves. He traced the outline of her lips with a delicate finger and raised her chin, coming closer so that Mary's heart began a familiar race. "Let them speculate, let them say the worst, for they will," Justin whispered. "All they need know is how perfectly matched we are! Let them be jealous of our happiness and love, and make of that what they will!"

Now his fingers traced the outline of her face and neck, followed the hollow of her throat, which he kissed, then Justin looked up and smiled. All Mary could see were his eyes, gentle and loving, the parted lips as he came closer.

He whispered huskily, lips almost touching, "*Let us seal this contract…*"

"…Did you not hear me, girl? Cook has gone to bed with a fever, and there's no one else to lay the supper!"

Emily was standing over her. That look of disapproval was worn as easily as her black fustian, Mary thought. She didn't respond to her mother's complaints and instead brushed back her hair and drew the heddle up and under, up and under, until another row was finished and the cross transect with its halo was done.

"Cook is sick and could not go to market! I fear there's

not even a stone to make soup with!" Emily wailed.

"Shall I go to The Castle and Motte, Mother?" Mary asked. "Perhaps Mister Lawton will have a roasted hen and potatoes."

"Yes–but make certain you say it's for yourself and not me."

"Of course, Mother. There's no sense shaming both of us."

"Be sure it's a good hen, and the potatoes are golden brown, roasted, no charring, and soft. And if he has some fresh bread, ask for it–and ale," Emily said as she followed Mary around as shawl and purse were fetched. "And be sure to take the path into Knowstone, don't go through the abbey. I know you like to walk there—ah, it's almost dark! Have Gordon take you in the trap—Mary! Are you listening?"

"No need to disturb Gordon at his supper. I can walk to the village."

"You most certainly will not! We have the means."

"An even better reason. We're no better than anyone else in Knowstone despite what people whisper. I'll be home shortly with your supper."

Mary closed the door behind her and took in a great breath of cool, twilight air crisp with the scent and smoke of hearth fires. She was glad to be out and her journey ahead. Knowstone was a mile away from Hazelwick, the crumbling, ancient manor Emily had purchased with the legacy left to her after Percy's death. Hazelwick lay in the park beyond St. Edmund Wood and was far enough away from the gossips and crones of Knowstone that it gave Mary peace—at least on the walks to and from the village.

She listened to the gentle crunch of her shoes on the path beaten by generations of travelers, leaves crackling, and the scud of her heels on the earth. A deer watched her from a safe distance, poised to fly if Mary changed her direction. The last of the day's sunlight shot amber rays through the trees and speckled the path, shining on the ancient gate of the more ancient, ruined abbey that stood at the edge of the wood as a boundary between Hazelwick and the outskirts of Knowstone. Before her soared the spires and skeletal remains, the traceries of the gothic abbey buildings. Going through the abbey was the shortest route to the village. She hesitated, staring at the gate, and reached for the latch. Looking down, she remembered Justin's hand on hers.

"...of what are you so afraid?"

The gate creaked open and thudded close behind them. Mary's eyes darted toward the abbey ruins before them and then back to Justin. "I'd rather go another way back to the village."

"We've been gone too long, and your mother will have begun to worry."

Mary took a furtive step and looked down at her boot scuffing against what used to be a paving stone in the chapter house, the ochre and rose-colored stone displaying the edge of a trefoil pattern. She looked up at Justin, smiling tenderly at her. "You will think it's childish," she sighed. "It is said the abbey is haunted. They are ghosts of nuns who were defiled and murdered by the Normans when they came here after the Conquest."

"Now come, I won't let anything hurt you."

With his arm around her waist and her hand clasped in his, Mary and Justin walked on, pausing to admire the skeletal remains of barrel vaulting and clerestory, the shards of a stained glass window pouring colored light onto the greenwood.

"I think in a past life you were a noblewoman. Noblewomen were abbesses and held great sway in society and at court. They were sought after for their intellect, their wealth, some for their beauty–you would be such a prize!"

"Oh really, Justin!"

"You are meant to be in a castle on a hilltop by the sea."

They paused to watch the sunset, and leaning against him, Mary felt his lips on her neck. She relaxed as his hands glided up from her waist to rest just below her breasts, and he held her against him.

"Mary!" he whispered. "*I will marry you! Your father will hear me out, I swear it, my dearest!*"

The sudden departure of a bird brought her attention to an overgrowth in what used to be the nave of the abbey church. Beyond that were a fore gate and a path overgrown by gooseberries and long grass that led to Knowstone.

Mary paused by the tabernacle to the Virgin that had survived the centuries of disuse. It mattered little that the Blessed Mother had lichen and dirt in the folds of her dress and spattered on her limestone face, making her painted eyes more luminous, if not frightening. Mary plucked a few wildflowers, laying them at the Virgin's moss-encrusted feet.

"Lady Mother, do you know what it's like to be alone in the entire world?" Mary whispered.

"Best not to be in places like this alone."

The growl made Mary start, and she gasped, short of a scream. Turning, she was close, eye to eye with Abraham Creetur. He carried a bow with arrows, a brace of coneys slung over his shoulder.

"Sunset soon, Miss. Best be going back to the manor," he muttered, hobbling off.

"Thank you!" Mary called after him. Somewhere a bird rustled and chirruped, then took flight. Mary pulled her shawl tighter and hurried along the path until she could see the lights flickering one by one in the windows of Knowstone.

Simon the Lamplighter was already climbing his ladder up and down Whitecastle Street, leaving behind him great orange and yellow flames in the glass lamps. Mary was surprised when he called to her and let tuppence sail through the air. "Forgive me, Mistress! I never gave you a wedding gift!" he explained when Mary looked up, holding the coin.

"You shouldn't. What if you need it?"

"I can look to myself, Mistress," the lamplighter replied, pulling respectfully on his cap and scrambling down his ladder, hitching it under his arm and moving on to the next lamp.

Mary basked in this kindness for only a moment. She was still staring at the copper wonder of the two-penny coin when she felt the sting of an insect on her cheek. She slapped and found that her hand came away red, looked down, and saw the pebbles. Looking round, she saw the children across the lane. They were shouting at her as another volley of stones was loosed, hitting their mark accurately. One of the stones struck her forehead sharply. Almost immediately, she felt the warm trickle of blood in her hair and above her brows. Then came the jeers and taunts, the filthy names boys learned from their fathers when they shouldn't be listening.

"Here, you brats! Leave off! Go home and make your mothers miserable!" Simon shouted. He slid down the ladder and came at the boys waving an oil pot with a yellow flame dancing out of the lip. As he ran past Mary, a spark lit on her forehead, and the acrid smell of burning hair made her reach up to feel the burn of the flame against her fingers. She cried out, and Simon was back at her side, patting out the singed hair too late. "Now see what you've made me do, you bastards!" Simon growled at the boys.

"T'was your pot, not ours!" one of the boldest boys scoffed, and for good measure, he threw a rock that missed Mary's head and shattered a windowpane behind her. That alone made the boys scatter, screaming in fright, doors slamming shut behind them.

"I'm alright," Mary said to the unasked question apparent on Simon's face. The shop owner behind the broken window only glowered at her and at his damaged window, looking accusingly at Simon, who muttered apologies and went about his work. Mary found a kerchief in her purse and pressed it against her forehead as she hurried up the street. The taunts and names were still with her when she found sanctuary in The Castle and Motte.

"Oh Lord, Miss!" Dorcas exclaimed when Mary dropped wearily into a booth. She brought a wet cloth to wipe away the blood, a glass of whiskey to dull the pain.

"It's nothing, Dorcas," Mary protested. She knew all eyes were upon her, and behind their tankards were mocking smiles. "I want a roasted hen and potatoes, some carrots if you have them ready. Cook's down with a fever, and there's nothing."

"Dorcas!" The Innkeeper snapped.

"Sir?"

"We don't want trouble. You know the rules, my girl!"

"Master Lawton," Mary rasped, trying to fight the tears stinging the abrasions on her face, the painful throbbing of her forehead, the burned skin below her hairline. "Cook's down with a fever. There's nothing in the pantry."

"Learn to tell time, Miss, or didn't they teach you that in Oxford with the music and art, and philosophy? Supper's done!"

"I have money enough! I'll pay eight shillings! A whole angel, if I must!"

"Master Lawton," Godwin Herrold spoke up from his usual table in his usual corner, behind the usual piles of papers and books. He was busy making notes on a page and didn't bother looking up. "Perhaps you didn't hear Mister Talbot's sermon last week? Whatsoever you do to the least of my brothers that you do unto me? You would not dispute that a widow or orphan, a young woman, deserves the same as one of Christ's more fortunate brothers or sisters, such as the Merrows or Frankewells?"

"We can't go changing the rules for just anyone," Lawton groused. "Especially those who think they're better than most!" This last was directed at Mary, who was wiping away new tears and blood with her shawl's hem.

"All I want is supper! Is it so much to ask?" Mary cried with exasperation.

"Lawton?" Godwin queried as he continued to write.

Sighing, Lawton waved at Dorcas, and she ran to the kitchen, shouting orders. Moments later, a kitchen boy lugged a provisioned basket that was dropped on the floor with a thud a few feet from Mary as if it were alms for a leper.

Mary sniffed back tears and nodded her thanks. Leaving The Castle and Motte, she wanted to shake the dust from her shoes and never come back but knew that would be impossible. On her way to the door, she hesitated by Godwin's table. Godwin, engrossed in his sermon notes, turned to open a commentary, finally glanced up, saw her, and noticed the scrapes and cuts. He was on his feet in a moment, fumbling for his handkerchief. Before he could offer it, she was gone, the door slamming shut.

"What is wrong with all of you that you should treat her so severely?" Godwin shouted. He didn't expect an answer and was actually relieved when he received none. When the patrons returned to their card games, conversations and drink, Godwin barked for more wine.

"You've had enough, Father," Dorcas admonished, taking away his cup.

"Then send a bottle to wherever Mistress Burnley goes. Do not say where it came from. Here's money. Go on, girl!"

Dorcas grabbed the money Godwin shoved at her and glanced behind her only once as she fled, taking one of the best bottles of wine.

Out in Whitecastle Street, Dorcas saw Mary struggling with the basket as she made her way out of the village. She caught her up and smiled when Mary looked up in amazement at the sound of her name, clutching her shawl about her face.

"Let me, Miss. I can go with you to Hazelwick," Dorcas offered. "That basket's too heavy. We can carry it together."

Dorcas took one of the handles and, tucking the bottle inside the basket, set off towards the wood.

"Thank you," Mary said after they'd walked a half-mile or so.

"No need to thank me, Miss! Besides, those brats won't be back—leastwise, not until tomorrow if there are two of us. They're always causing trouble. You just happened to be their quarry tonight. Tomorrow it will be poor Mistress Galthwaite or her cat."

"The cat doesn't deserve such treatment."

Dorcas pondered that for a moment and then laughed aloud, which brought a rare smile to Mary's lips. "There, Miss! That's how I remember you before you went away," Dorcas said.

"I didn't ask for wine," Mary commented.

"No, you didn't, Miss, and more than like Mister Lawton wouldn't have spared a flask of vinegar for you. This here's a gift from a gentleman."

Dorcas saw Mary's nod in the twilight. "When you return to Knowstone, Dorcas, you may thank the vicar for his kindness."

CHAPTER 4

THE SCARS ON Mary's face were apparent but not disfiguring. Emily wondered why the girl thought nothing of them, for men would surely take account. And her hair! The burned hair was sheared off in a fringe above her eyebrows like that of a medieval page boy! Well, at least the scars and burn welts on her forehead were hidden—but Mary did have such lovely skin and a high, proud brow that set off her beautiful, large eyes. What a pity it all was. If Mary wanted to find another husband, she would have to take greater care of her appearance. The girl rarely glanced in a mirror. Nor did she wear a bonnet or carry a parasol when she went out, which was every day, and she looked like a gypsy girl with the windblown hair, her tan face, and hands.

"I wonder why you do not speak to the parents of those brats," Emily sniffed as she watched Mary fold yards of fair linen and place it in a basket.

"It would do no good. If not the children throwing stones, then surely the parents. I do not wonder at that."

"Then you should denounce them!"

"Shall I stand on the market cross and make a proclamation, Mother? Who would come to my defense? Who would be my champion?" Mary sighed. "People would jeer and laugh, be derisive, I would be called a great many things, most of which would not be true."

"I am sure you would be better situated if you returned to London or Oxford."

"And there I should be no trouble for you."

"Mary! I said nothing—!"

"How unfortunate that Justin's parents are dead—I

would have been welcomed in Liverpool."

"Are you saying that I hold no affection for you, Mary? You are my daughter!"

"I am your burden," Mary said as she opened the door.

"Where do you go now?" Emily whined.

"To market, and then to St. Ælfgiva's. It's Saturday, Mother."

"Ah! You shouldn't trouble Mister Talbot. It would be better to take your linens to Crewe or Chester, where you'd fetch a good price–a better price than here. He doesn't appreciate your work as it is."

"Well," Mary sighed, "At least St. Ælfgiva's knows the quality of my needlework and weaving and depends on our arrangement. Were I to ply my trade in Crewe or Chester, I could easily find myself living on the streets for lack of money, for I'd have no clients. Would you like that, Mother?"

Before Emily could offer several warnings or shove a parasol in her hands, Mary was gone.

The church of St. Ælfgiva's and its vicarage stood at the western end of Whitecastle Street, close by the market and guildhall. The church and its great medieval cross could be seen from Mary's bedroom window at Hazelwick. So too could she see beyond the church to a tributary of the River Dee, the roads toward London and Wales, the ruins of one of the many castles put here in the days of Edward Longshanks, and the outcropping of forest that marked the Welsh border. How many mornings had she sat by the window combing out her hair and wondering if she should take one of those roads? The journey into Wales, she thought, would be less onerous than the stroll through Knowstone Market.

Mary headed east toward the market cross and was thankful the streets were mostly empty. The dinner hour approached. When she noticed The Young Clergyman passing through the church lych-gate, Mary brought her head up, and rather than go along at a steady clip with head down as was her usual custom, she took her time and met glance for glance, stare for stare. She would not allow him to see her vulnerable to the opinion of Knowstone. Besides, the scars were on the face. They wouldn't see those etched on her heart.

Mrs. Galthwaite's Holland tulips were growing nicely, as were the foxgloves and roses. The gardener herself curtly nodded when Mary passed and looked up from her hedgerow.

"Mistress Burnley. How is your mother?" Mrs. Galthwaite demanded, stabbing at the earth with a trowel.

"Well enough," Mary answered.

Mrs. Galthwaite sat up on her knees and frowned. "Don't we look proud! That pale pink is best suited for a virgin, Mistress Burnley. And such a fashion! Where is your bonnet, child? Your fichu? And no corsets!"

"I'll mark that in my book this evening: corsets, bonnet, fichu, and I should not wear pink. I must tell you, ma'am, that no one of good society has worn a fichu for almost twenty years. Anything else I should mark?"

"Better manners, I think!"

"Good afternoon, Mistress Galthwaite."

Mr. Rede, the baker, removed the gooseberry pies and sweet buns cooling on the counter just as Mary's shadow passed the door. She placed a new shilling on a worn spot of the wood in exchange for a half-dozen sweet buns. "Nice to see you, Mistress," Mr. Rede grumbled, avoiding the disapproving stares of passersby.

"Good of you to say so," Mary remarked and bit into the savory sweetness of a warm bun, continued on her way.

The window display at the dressmaker's shop caught Mary's eye as she passed. Few things in a dress shop ever caught Mary's fancy, but that afternoon she could not tear herself away.

An evening frock of pale apricot silk stood on a mannequin with a matching pelisse. The fabric was unique in that it was decorated with embroidered gold stars and was iridescent, the light making the fabric apricot at one moment, golden another. The *décolleté* neckline, high waistline, and short cap sleeves were still all the rage in fashionable London society.

Mary wanted it, *décolleté* and all. She'd forsake her ideals and standards for that dress, to wear it in London or Oxford, even here in Knowstone, where they knew nothing about everything.

"Yes, this is the frock I told you about, Caroline! From Paris, I'm sure."

Two women and their children had paused to gape in the windows and were now gasping and cooing at the dresses and bonnets, slippers, gloves, and shawls, on display.

"Surely, Paris! Look at the handiwork on the hems. The stars! One might think they really did twinkle," the second woman chattered, her nose pressed against the window glass to see better and block sunlight reflected on the panes.

"And the pelisse! What do you think? Woolen or velvet? Yes, this must be from Paris."

"No, from London," Mary now offered. "I saw something like this in London, at a concert. The Duchess of Norfolk wore a dress exactly like this. I remember . . . I remember that everyone in the house admired her, and my husband said he wished he could afford such a gown for me."

The women turned, recognizing Mary immediately. Without another word, they each took a child by the hand and led them away.

Mary sadly watched them go and then returned to her vigil on the dress. Yes, she *had* seen the Duchess of Norfolk in this dress! It was Christmas last. Justin had given her two frocks in this latest fashion.

"*We are the makers of fashion, my dear.*"

"But Justin, can we afford these? The work alone must have cost a pound, if not more!"

"I've taken two students on, and I'm writing for the Historical Society, so yes, my love, we can very much afford to dress you in the latest fashion."

"Which one shall I wear to the Christmas Ball, then?"

"The saffron. You will be iridescent."

Mary melted into his arms and kissed him. "Have there ever been two people happier, my love?" she whispered.

"*Never…*"

"It's a beautiful thing, is it not?"

The woman's voice startled Mary out of her daydream, and she looked around and saw Maeve Pinkerton, lady's maid to Isobel Frankewell. She was a cold, humorless woman. The way she carried herself and her deportment took away from the beauty of her face and form, for Maeve held herself in high regard despite the fact no one else did.

"It is beautiful," Mary answered and glanced at Maeve, offering a smile and nodding towards the dress, continued, "You would do this much justice, Miss Pinkerton, for the color suits your eyes."

"I thank you, Mistress Burnley, but it is too proud and beautiful a thing for the likes of Knowstone!"

"What are the likes of Knowstone, I wonder?" Mary commented.

"Strange question you ask, since you of all people would know: a provincial, unkind, unloving place."

"There are some good qualities. Is the castle not beautiful in its ruins? The houses and streets are well kept, and most of the villagers have the Gospel in their hearts."

Maeve took a step closer and offered a malicious smile. "And what of Erland Frankewell? Is he not a boon? Is he not one of Knowstone's best qualities? Certainly that is the exact reason you're here and not in Oxford. Someone with common sense would never give returning a second thought."

"A person must have a home."

"There are houses in Oxford."

Mary offered a curtsey and turned to go, then spun around, saying, "Often we do not have choices, and so we return to the familiar against our own desires. We are reminded of our faults and never praised for our achievements. We are constantly reminded by quizzical looks and pointed suggestions that men like Erland Frankewell are suitable for neither maid nor vicar's daughter no matter how much we try to persuade ourselves otherwise."

"He chose you, Mary."

Now it was Mary's turn to smile. "Despite your best efforts to persuade him otherwise. You may renew your claim upon him. You shall not have a rival in me, Miss Pinkerton."

"And yet you wear the necklace he gave you even now." Maeve gestured with a gloved finger at the diamond pendant around Mary's neck, which made the other girl's face blush angrily, and a trembling hand clasped the tear-drop stone.

"Good day to you, Maeve Pinkerton."

"Good day," Maeve said as they both curtseyed and went their ways—Maeve into the dressmaker's shop and Mary to St. Ælfgiva's.

The tenth-century church had always been Mary's favorite place in Knowstone. Most thought it a dark and depressing place despite the restored stained glass windows—its chief beauty—but Mary found something more than beauty in the remnants of Anglo-Saxon architecture and the Norman additions, the smooth walls with its peeling, fading frescoes uncovered after centuries of neglect and disgrace; the pale, sweet faces of saints and angels staring down at her from the midst of plaster.

She found serenity.

Mary walked to the foot of the sanctuary steps and waited. It was five o'clock, and she was late. The altar guild ladies always met her at half-past four to discuss the linen needs of the church.

The ambulatory door opened, and Godwin Herrold came out with a prayer book and candlesticks, bringing them to the altar. He made an obeisance and, as he turned, noticed Mary. She took a step backward and stared as if she'd seen a ghost.

The light from the windows shone down on his face. It was a sad countenance yet with bright hair and light eyes, almost as if he'd stepped out of one of the frescoes over the altar. He was young, closer to her age than Justin had been. For all his youth, he looked weary and troubled.

He was the most handsome man she'd ever seen; if a man could be beautiful, here was proof! Mary felt the color rise in her cheeks when he looked at her. His eyes burned into her, and he stared the way the other men did. Mary was used to this gaze borne of lust and desire to possess her body and soul, but it made her uncomfortable with this man.

"Good evening, Mistress," he said at last. The voice was soft and deep. Mary was pleased. Often the voice and the man did not go together. He came forward now and smiled in greeting. Mary shied away from this giant towering over her. He was well proportioned and looked like a medieval knight.

"Is Mistress Renfrew here?" she asked.

"May I help you? Do you require alms?"

She sighed. "No, I do not! Why does everyone suppose I require charity? I have brought the fair cloth," Mary demanded, exasperated.

"Fair cloth, Mistress?"

"Yes. I've furnished the linens for nearly five months now since returning home."

Here she knelt and uncovered her market basket, taking from it three folded squares of embroidered white on white linen, unfurling and holding them out for inspection. She sighed again when he failed to notice the linen.

"Perhaps Saint Andrew's in Barkingham will have need of these."

"I didn't—forgive me, Mistress! You've taken pains."

Now he took the cloth from Mary and inspected it, looking from time to time at Mary, who stared at him, just as curious.

"Your courtesy surprises me, Sir."

"Why is that?"

"I've come to expect a most unkind reception in Knowstone. Everyone has an opinion of me, and not at all kind."

"And who are you that I should know you? I can see

you're an excellent seamstress and weaver. That is all I need to know."

"I am Mary Burnley, the Reverend Percy Witherslack's daughter." When he did not respond, Mary continued: "Does that not give you pause, sir? Are you not concerned?" She nodded toward the fair linen when he still did not respond. "Mistress Renfrew pays a half-crown for each, sir."

"A half-crown for each? So little for so much! I've seen cloth as fine as this at Canterbury Cathedral."

"Half-crown. Yes. Shall I come tomorrow to settle the account?"

"Mister Talbot will be here after supper, for Evening Prayer, if you would wait."

"I'd rather return tomorrow. He would prefer to see me in sackcloth and ashes or walk through Knowstone stripped to the waist and carrying only a candle!"

The reference to medieval punishment for women of ill repute made Godwin suddenly laugh. "How unlike the others you are! You are like the clean air after a storm."

"But I am not. Good day, Mister.…"

"Godwin. Godwin Herrold."

"Mister Herrold."

Mary took her basket, made an obeisance, and left quietly.

He folded his arms across his chest, still holding the fair linen, and watched until she was lost in the blinding light of the open door. The scent of wildflowers that she brought with her still lingered.

"Everything in readiness for evening prayer, Godwin?"

Charles Talbot's voice startled Godwin, and he moved guiltily away from the altar. Talbot noticed the cloth still in Godwin's hands and came forward. "What have you there? Don't tell me those stupid sluts from the village have burned holes in the fair linen again!"

"It is fair linen, sir. Mistress Burnley brought it. Half-crown for each. Most excellent workmanship, such as I've never seen. A rare blessing."

"Blessing it is not. That is something you may drop wax upon or burn!"

"Burn it? But I don't understand,"

"Burn the cloth or give it back, but I'd rather you burn it. Well? Do as you're told. You're not Archbishop of Canterbury yet!"

Talbot walked back the way he came, through the ambulatory and sacristy, and once the door banged shut and echoed through the nave, Godwin followed the same path but closed the door more quietly and went into the sacristy. He held the linen over the dust bin for only a moment and then shoved it into the back of a small cupboard that had been in disuse for years.

∞

"THE GRACE OF our Lord Jesus Christ, and the love of God, and the fellowship of the Holy Ghost be with us all evermore."

"Amen."

Seven heads bobbed to the processional cross as Godwin and his acolyte processed out of the nave and down the center aisle. Only one person did not offer courtesy, and that was Mary Burnley, sitting off in the dark shadows of the dimly-lit church, the purple light of dusk in her hair. The others left quietly, another evening prayer service done, whispering to one another and smiling back at Godwin as he took their alms.

"Do you believe all that you said, Mister Herrold?"

Godwin was closing the church doors and all but slammed them shut at the unexpected sound of her voice.

"Mistress Burnley! I was told you did not, that is, I mean to say, you would not…"

She stood and came from her bench, a prayer book in one hand, roses in another. "That is to say, you have been told a great many things, I am certain."

"Yes."

His head was bowed shamefully as she approached. Thinking that she would come closer, he involuntarily closed his eyes and whispered a prayer. When he opened them, she was placing roses at the feet of an ancient statue of the Virgin and Child, a relic of the old religion that had been saved by the people of Knowstone in the days of Henry VIII and was a curiosity for travelers to pause and marvel at en route to Wales. She once stood in the abbey. The proof of her worth was the alms box that was always full of shillings, tuppence, and thruppence, a pound or two.

"Well, I am here."

Godwin frowned.

"To collect for the linens?" she asked, smiling. The smile he added to an expanding list of her virtues.

"Ah! Come."

He could hear her quick steps on the flagstones as she followed him over the graves of the ancient and illustrious of Knowstone buried under the church floor, past the tomb of an unknown knight and his lady, through the sanctuary and into the ambulatory and sacristy. Godwin unlocked a drawer and sorted through coins, and carefully placed them in her palm. "A half-crown each, which would make a pound for eight linens, I believe?"

"Shall I bring more next month, sir?"

"If you like."

"Then I shall." A pause, then: "You didn't answer my question, Mister Herrold—if you believed what you preached."

"I believe that Christ died for our sins if that is what you want to know."

"Why then do people continue to sin? Does Christ need to be sacrificed every day so that we may live without sin?"

"We remember His sacrifice when we receive Holy Communion. We remember His new commandment and honor it every time we break bread and take the cup and share it. His words are but a paraphrasing of that which His ancestors spoke when they recalled their deliverance from Egypt and reminds us that His coming to Earth was for but one purpose: to take our sins and transgressions upon His shoulders. It is our deliverance out of Egypt."

"What if he came to Earth to show us a new way to live? A way to love one another as he loved us?" Mary asked, coming closer. "I still do not understand, Mister Herrold, that if we are washed white and new in the blood of the Lamb, and are free of sin, then why do people continue to sin? To hate and to do harm to one another? That is what I want to know."

"I don't know." This was said after a long, painful moment while Godwin studied the perfect face staring up at him. A face so exquisitely beautiful and enchanting it had been in his mind's eye for weeks. The lips he had no thought of but to kiss and kiss again.

"Let me posit this, sir, if I may."

"Of course."

"Could it be that we were gifted with Free Will? That man will always want and want, and it never be enough? And that all a woman ever wants to is to have her say, and perhaps to be given her own way if the argument is sound?" She frowned and looked as if studying the pattern of shadows on the floor. Her eyes were raised and then dropped to her sides. "It is all I have ever wanted."

"I'm sorry, Mistress Burnley. I don't know."

"At least you are honest, which is more than can be said for many. God keep you safe this night," she said.

"Mistress Burnley!"

She turned, her eyes questioning.

"I do not know why Mister Talbot will have none of your work but continue to bring it, but on Wednesday evenings. He is in Chester on Wednesdays."

"We have an agreement then," she said, nodding and the hint of a smile crossing her lips.

"May I accompany you home? It's late, and…"

"I can find my way, sir, but I thank you. Besides, Mister Lawton will have laid your supper in The Castle and Motte, and you wouldn't want it going to spoil, would you?"

Another smile, and she was on her way.

Godwin watched the hems of her skirts as she passed

through the church door. He walked down the nave, picking up prayer books and hymnals, stacking them neatly at the ends of pews. At the statue of the Virgin and Child, Godwin paused and took one of the roses, inhaling its perfume. Then he reached out and touched the cold, Purbeck marble face that seemed to glow with life.

CHAPTER 5

MARY'S TALENT AS a weaver and seamstress wasn't favored by Charles Talbot, but it was appreciated by Charlotte Wainwright, who commissioned a christening wardrobe for her infant son Henry. Such a business transaction would have gone unnoticed had the child been someone other than Sir Martin Frankewell's first grandson.

Sir Martin was the district's only landed gentry. Lady Isobel, his finely boned, frail-looking wife, was the youngest daughter of the Earl of Salisbury. Though Lady Isobel looked as if a good wind would snap her in two, she proved sturdy enough to bear Martin's five sons and two daughters. No one knew what Lady Isobel thought, for she was the most circumspect of women in Knowstone. When she did speak, it was an event, and the housewives gossiped for weeks about Lady Isobel's considerable opinions. The only woman who could equal her was the young lady who now stood in the morning room of Saltfield Manor and quietly listened as praise was heaped on her.

Lady Isobel ran a finger along a delicate line of stitching on the tiny christening cap in her hand. "Your talent is wasted here, Mary. You should return to London. The ladies at Court would give you their custom and at a better price than what is offered here in the Northwest." When Mary did not answer, she added, with one of her rare smiles, "I know what you're thinking: I have offended you by supposing you are nothing more than a shopkeeper, and women from your place in society are not expected to keep shops."

"It isn't my place in society to let others know what I'm thinking, Lady Isobel."

Another smile graced those perfect red lips, and then Lady Isobel laughed, her delighted reaction bringing her eldest son, Erland, to the morning room door. He looked in, and when Mary turned at the sound of his boots, he departed just as quickly, never bothering to find out what amused his mother.

"You shall do well to spite all of us!" Lady Isobel laughed.

"I only wish to make my living and to be left alone."

This admission sobered Lady Isobel, and she nodded. Now she placed a hand on Mary's cheek, and out of the corner of her eye, Mary could see the brilliant diamonds in her wedding band. "Dearest Mary, I regret all that has happened. But know this: it had to be done. I pray you will forgive me?"

Mary smiled sadly. "You've done nothing that requires forgiveness. I beg your forgiveness," she whispered.

"It is given. Now, do come and see us again. We have missed you all these months!"

"I shall try, Lady Isobel."

"Do you have the books I gave you? Edmund Spencer and Donne? Petrarch?"

"Yes, and I thank you."

"Good. Ah, you still wear the diamond I gave you for your sixteenth birthday!"

"I treasure it. It is a friend."

"And I am your true friend."

"Thank you."

Mary was dismissed then, and as she left, Lady Isobel said, "Never give up hope, Mary Burnley. That alone sustains us."

Erland was tucked into a window seat and reading when Mary passed through the salon to the staircase. She dipped into a neat curtsey and forced a smile when he glanced up. He was on his feet in a second with the courtliest of bows.

"I have kept the volume of sonnets you gave me," Erland spoke up and showed the book in his hands. After a moment of studying her, he asked, "How are you, Mary?"

"Well. As you see me."

"Uncommonly beautiful as always."

"I believe that would be the fault of my parents."

"And always clever." The book was snapped shut and tossed on the window seat. "Perhaps more thanks to a year at university with a husband, surrounded by the best minds and the most adoring friends."

"Why is it thought I attended university? And if it were so, why should that be a fault or something to be ashamed of?"

"Because my dear," Erland walked towards her, his eyes locked on hers, "it is bad enough to possess a beauty that men cannot have, worse still to be more intelligent than those who worship you and dream of you, and want you in their beds."

Mary was ready to speak but thought better of it, made another curtsey, eyes downcast, and moved around him to leave the room. As she passed, he brushed a hand lightly across her cheek and watched the gentle sway of her hips and the shawl floating off her shoulders as she went.

The encounter put him in an excellent mood. A moment in Mary's presence did that. Erland threw himself back onto the window seat and picked up the book of sonnets. "Shall I compare thee to a summer's day," he read aloud.

"You know it will be the greatest sin of your life if you renew that courtship or think to use her."

His mother's voice spoiled the moment.

Erland glanced over at Isobel and offered a smile he knew would soften that hard line of her porcelain jaw and remove the flint from her violet eyes. Of all her sons, Erland resembled Isobel the most. From the fairest of gilt blond hair, darkest blue eyes, so blue they appeared violet, and the stature and carriage of their ancestors, the ancient Danes: the tall, beautiful, Northmen who conquered and settled in England before William the Bastard had even been born.

"Do you know me so well, Mother?" Erland asked. "Because if you did, you'd know that it would be the least!"

Isobel was about to speak but exhaled those words with a sigh and went back to her parlor.

∞

NO MATTER LADY Isobel's kind disposition toward Mary, she was not invited to Saltfield for Henry's christening. Mary stayed home as if it were any other day and as soon as her mother hurried off, spent most of the day at the loom, leaving the house only to stretch her limbs and soothe an aching back. Her innocent search for freedom from tedium started a row of the worst kind when Emily returned home late in the afternoon, eager to gossip with her daughter. She was disappointed when she returned and found the girl gone. At a quarter past five o'clock, the door closed with a slam, and Emily assumed her most indignant pose.

"Where've you been, girl? I want to tell you about the christening party." Emily's was not a question but a demand. She glanced over her copy of *Punch* and sighed, noting the muddy hems of Mary's frock and petticoats. "Look at you! Even at twenty years of age, you refuse to look respectable. The milkmaids at Charleston's dairy spend more time before a looking glass than you—ah! Now there's a pain I've not felt before! Give me my shawl. The ride to Saltfield and back must have given me a chill. The shawl, girl!"

Mary dutifully brought a woolen shawl from the settee and draped it over her mother's lap. For a moment, their eyes met. Mary removed her glance quickly and if Emily hadn't seized her arm, would have escaped into the far parlor.

"Do you know what is being said?" Emily growled. "The most unkind of things! The very worst kind of things! And you are being made a whore, a slut!"

Their eyes, similar in shape and size but not in color nor clarity, now locked. Mary gently wrested free of her mother's grasp and rubbed the sore spot on her forearm where a bruise would rise by morning.

"How fortunate for you. Had I been painted a martyr or saint in their imaginations, what would you have to say?"

"Remember yourself, my girl! You are not a mistress of Oxford here!"

I never was, to begin with, Mary thought as she retreated to her sanctuary of the far parlor. *What would they all think if they knew the truth?*

Soon the house echoed with the slow, comfortable rhythm of the loom; Mary was lost in the routine of leading the bobbins back and forth across the warp threads, a song from her childhood in her head that kept time with the beats of the heddle against the new fabric. Even Cook and the maid hummed along as they went about their chores. Emily spent the hour before dinner settling into her discontent. She glanced about her parlor and sighed. It was not what she had wanted.

Emily was by no means destitute. She lived comfortably on her widow's pension, and she had inherited a comfortable sum of seventy-two pounds and seven from her brother. Her house was large, and she kept two servants. The furnishings were immaculate, simple, evidence of the owner's desire to be better placed in society. Just last Christmas, her sister in Chester gave her a new pianoforte, which now held the place of honor in the great parlor where she held court. The mantle over the hearth in the sitting room was cluttered with trinkets and framed portraits. The stairwell was decorated with paintings of ancestors, all of them dour and oppressed. Emily Witherslack knew she was out of place in this rustic backwater, this rural setting of use only to watercolor artists. She had been born to a respectable London family with an equally respectable fortune and place in society. With this thought in mind, Emily soon nodded off to sleep, quite certain her daughter's shameful life had brought her to old age early.

What her daughter thought was of no moment.

"Oh dear, Miss—she's fallen asleep again! The lamb roast will spoil if you wait," Cora the Maid sighed after discovering Emily snoring in her chair. Mary had entered the parlor when she noticed her mother's absence from the dining room and now stood beside the maid and considered what should be done.

"Leave her be," Mary finally said. "You know how cross she'll be if you wake her. She'll have a tray in her room when she wakes."

For the first time in months, dinner was pleasant and quiet for all concerned. Without Emily's constant harping and complaints, Mary ate an entire meal, and Cora had no reason to fly from the dining room in tears.

"Cora, your apron is frayed," Mary commented when she looked up as the dishes were taken away. "And your dress is twice turned, is it not?"

Cora blushed and wiped her hands on a worn patch of the apron. "I've almost saved enough for a new frock, Miss. I'm sorry. Mistress Witherslack chides me so about the way I look, but it isn't a fault of mine. Cook and I haven't seen a month of wages."

Mary shoved away from the dish of fruit placed before her and left the room, returning minutes later with a handful of coins that she pressed into Cora's unsuspecting hands.

"This should be enough for two good dresses and an apron. And your livery. If Cook needs anything, tell her to come to me."

"Thank you, Miss!" Cora cried and took a step closer to embrace Mary for her kindness and thought better of it. She made a neat curtsey and hurried out. While Mary finished her meal, she smiled as she listened to the excited and happy conversation between The Cook and Cora. One of them had a suitor.

It had been some time since Mary heard laughter in the house.

The moment of happiness lasted only a while longer. After dinner, Mary brought her mending to the kitchen and enjoyed the company of Cora and The Cook while they did the cleaning up, and she darned her best stockings. The pleasant warmth of the hearth, the sound of the pots and pans clattering, and the occasional conversation about everyday things, little things, were comforting. With every stitch, Mary relaxed and told herself it was a good decision coming home…

"What's this?"

Cook and Cora bobbed down and up in curtsies as Emily entered the kitchen, her face sleep-heavy and cross. They barely glanced at the unfinished dishes in the sink and quietly disappeared up the back stairs while Emily watched just as quietly. As soon as they were gone, she strolled past the table, the countertops, and the hearth to make an inspection of this room she seldom visited.

"Have you no regard for your mother that you allow me to sleep through dinner and have no thought to see to my comfort?" Emily sighed, a hint of trembling in her voice.

"I instructed Cora to bring a tray once you'd been to your room. You were sleeping so soundly," Mary replied, not glancing up at her mother. "Would it not have been thoughtless to disturb your dreams?"

"You have the far parlor for *that!*" Emily responded, jabbing at the stocking. She took it in her hand and clucked her tongue in dissatisfaction, tossing it back. "There's no reason to hide here with the servants. Why do you waste your time on mending when a new pair costs little?"

"I only thought to leave you in peace. The light is much better here at this time of day, and to light the lamps in the far parlor seemed a waste of oil," Mary continued as she made several more careful stitches and then folded her work in her lap. Finally, she looked up at her mother and tried a smile that was met with a disapproving scowl.

"Ever the perfect daughter and child! I wonder what people would say if they knew the truth?"

With that, Emily marched out, the door to the stairwell slamming shut and echoing through the house. Mary waited a moment and then sighed, taking up the stocking and studying the almost invisible, perfect stitches. How she wished she could disappear into the fabric of life.

Indeed, she thought, w*hat would anyone do or say if they knew the truth?* She pondered that while washing the dishes.

"Here, now! Miss, you oughtn't to spend your evening doing this," Cook spoke up an hour later when she returned and found Mary stacking plates on the rack above the counter. She smiled nevertheless, for the kitchen was as spotless as it should be, as she, Cook, would make it.

"I had neither cook nor maid when we lived in Oxford and London," Mary replied, untying the apron and putting it carefully on a hook. "Of course, if I am intruding in any way, I'll stay clear," she added with a sweet, genuine smile.

"Oh, it's no bother to me, Miss," Cook replied as she lit a fire under the kettle and invited Mary to sit at the table. "It's Mistress Witherslack. If you don't mind my saying so, she goes out of her way to find fault with everyone and everything."

"True enough. I have no desire to make life difficult for you, Meg. Let's have our cup of tea and decide how we should go about our days, and we'll never say a word to her, shall we?"

The Cook nodded in agreement.

From that evening's conversation, a routine settled in the Witherslack household. Mary and The Cook conspired to be happy. As soon as it was light, Mary rose and helped Cook light the fires, start breakfast, and then shut herself up in the far parlor to work until noon, when she emerged flushed and exhausted to take a meal, listen to her mother's gossip, and then went out for a walk, returning at dusk. After supper with Emily, Mary returned to the parlor and worked well into the night.

It worked to Mary's satisfaction, and all was well until the afternoon Lady Isobel came unexpectedly to Hazelwick.

CHAPTER 6

SOMEONE KNOCKED AT the door, and Emily starting from her nap, called for Cora to see who it was.

"Lady Isobel! And Jane!" Emily exclaimed loudly. "My goodness, to think–why this is a surprise! To what should we owe this visit? Mary, Mary! Mary, come and see who's come to call!"

Mary continued the push the heddle and pass bobbins to and fro, watching a new pattern emerge. She threw the heddle harder as the voices rose and fell in polite, feminine conversation.

Emily was suddenly there in the parlor, pulling the curtain closed behind her. "Mary, put away your things!" she whispered excitedly and then giggled, adding, "This is quite unexpected! I did not think to have visitors ever again. Mary, Lady Isobel Frankewell, and Jane are here! And Mister Frankewell himself! Did you know that Jane is engaged to Lord Marchmont of Crewe's youngest son Robert—one hundred pounds per annum and a house in Bath! Three servants and a carriage and driver! And that is just in honor of the engagement! Mary! Do you hear me? Come at once!"

"Why should they want my company?" Mary's reply was bland and bored, her concentration on a warp thread that had gone askew.

"You think too highly of yourself to think they've come all this way for you! Perhaps they've not come to see you, my dear! And do not presume too much upon their kindness, Mary, but accept it, for you have none from any lady of standing in Knowstone! Now do come, and do something with your appearance–ah! Your boots! Where do you go, Girl, when you take your walks?"

Emily disappeared, sweetly chirping for Cook to bring refreshments worthy of the Frankewells.

By the time Mary came from the parlor, a proper tea had been spread, presided over by Emily. She simpered and giggled at their perplexed guests, instructing Cora in her most empirical voice to offer little cakes and sweetmeats and fragrant tea on the finest bone china plates and cups. Mary was appalled at the sight of Erland standing at the hearth with Maeve Pinkerton, who smiled sweetly and bobbed in a curtsey as she did the same.

"Here is Mary, Lady Isobel! Mary, come and greet Lady Isobel and Jane," Emily instructed. "And Mister Frankewell. It has been too long, Mister Frankewell, since you entered our little parlor!"

"As charming as ever," Erland pronounced. "Both the hostesses and the room."

"And Pinkerton. I've not seen you for weeks, for I believe you went on holiday to the continent?" Emily inquired. "Wasn't it when Mister Frankewell toured Italy and France to sketch antiquities?"

"Your memory is extraordinary, for that is correct," Maeve replied, glancing sideways at Erland, who was smirking and finding more entertainment stirring his tea and making the bowl ring with irritating notes, and then stopped when he noticed the frown creasing Mary's brow.

"Mary! Come and greet Lady Isobel and Jane!" Emily harped and let out a nervous laugh.

Jane Frankewell rose, smiling nervously, and wanted to embrace Mary, but Emily's darting eyes and scowl prompted her to think otherwise. They both came forward and greeted one another with awkward curtsies.

Mary now stood in the center of the great parlor–a schoolgirl waiting for her punishment. Twenty lines to be copied out in a neat, elegant cursive hand: '*I must conform, I must behave.*'

Jane refused to meet Mary's straightforward gaze. Jane was pretty but had not inherited the Frankewell beauty or social grace. More often than not, wealth and beauty did not go hand in hand, for if a young lady had a substantial dowry to offer, what else mattered? Mary and Jane complimented each other, and for reasons not quite certain to either, or dwelt upon, they had been close friends, almost sisters. Emily's eyes darted from one girl to the other and sighed, wondering why God had given her a daughter as beautiful as Mary when there was little else to commend her. Jane Frankewell was a dutiful, solemn, and quiet young lady. What all wives should be.

To Emily's horror, Isobel had no such qualms about greeting Mary with familiarity. She put aside her teacup and held out her hands.

"Child. Come and greet me with a kiss. And we must talk about London. You never spoke of it when you brought the christening clothes. Jane, here is our friend Mary. She looks well, doesn't she, Jane?"

"Remarkably, I think," Jane replied and now offered a genuine smile.

"Yes, a man's love often does that to a woman."

"Lady Isobel!" Emily tittered, embarrassed.

"There's a wooded garden, I see," Erland interrupted. "Pinkerton and I will explore Mary's celebrated roses and leave you to your private confidences. I'm sure you have much to discuss."

Mary's brow still wore its frown, and she glared as she watched them leave.

"How considerate of your son to take his leave when such a delicate subject is being discussed. And it's no business of a lady's maid to hear our conversation!" Emily sighed.

"You're scandalized, Emily? Why should you be? Let us speak plainly," Isobel admonished. "We are all women here. No, no, hear me out! We all pretend that love for us is unimportant, yet it is something we cannot live without. Mary has been to London and Oxford, and Athens, and for the life of me, I do not know why she returned to this miserable place!"

"She had no other place to go," Emily whined. "I am bound by my baptismal covenant to minister to widows and orphans, even if the widow is my daughter."

"Emily, the child is intelligent and clever. She must be if she can take the sweets from the tray right under our noses—and I think we all know what I mean." Isobel turned to Mary, saying, "Justin Burnley, I think, was the most handsome man of spirit and form as any I have ever seen."

"Thank you," Mary whispered.

"Am I right to suppose so, Mary?"

"Yes, Lady Isobel."

"Look at the child blush! She remembers something we will never know. She has known true pleasure, has lived the *Song of Songs*."

"Mary was raised to be a good Christian, Lady Isobel," Emily said. "For you to insinuate…"

"What insinuation do I make? I am only speaking the truth. She is too beautiful for widowhood. Find her a husband again, Emily!"

"For you to put ideas into her head, I meant!"

"Emily Witherslack, I may not be the widow of a vicar, but I do know more of what is most important in the world than you, who should, for all your piety and righteousness!" Isobel snapped. Jane and Mary both started in fright. "Do not hold that insufferable, questionable, perfect virtue of yours as something priceless, Emily! Learn something from your honest daughter. Look at her! It's written in her eyes. She did not find marriage a duty or the worst kind of punishment. She found pleasure where she ought to have."

"You are kind, Lady Isobel," Mary whispered.

"Mary. . ." Emily warned, glaring.

"Not kind, but honest. I have some inkling of the truth about you. We are alike in many ways, for we have been fortunate in our marriages, and many cannot say that," Isobel said, adding more gently then, "Oxford, Mary. How was

Oxford?"

"Large and wonderful. In Oxford, you are but one among many and not so much an oddity. It was like taking my first breath. Villages can be stifling and unkind places."

Here Emily made an exasperated sound and then smiled nervously at Isobel, who wagged her finger and said, "Do not fault the girl, Emily. She's one of the few who speaks her mind. Mary, I am truly sorry for the loss of Mister Burnley. He was a good man and a scholar of great merit but penniless and without means. That last, I think, was his only fault! I'm sorry to have only met him once."

Mary's face softened now and took on a new radiance, which the other women could not help but notice. "When was that?"

"He gave a lecture at the market hall—fourteenth-century nobility and personalities of the Lake District."

"Justin did so love the west country," Mary murmured.

Emily's brows rose, for she rarely heard her daughter speak her husband's name and so tenderly at that.

"He was a northern man, I hear?"

"A Lancashire man, Lady Isobel. From Liverpool."

"And his father was a cleric? His grandfather a professor of history?"

"Yes, Lady Isobel, but that would have been his mother's father. Justin was given his love of scholarship with his mother's milk. I am honored you would take pains to know something of him."

"It is my calling to know something of everyone." Now Isobel raked her eyes up and down Mary's curves and nodded. "You were ripe with a child!"

Jane now interceded on Mary's behalf, sensing her friend's discomfort. "Mary, we've come to ask for your service. I'm to be married and would like you to provide the linens for my trousseau and perhaps my dress? I know of no seamstress in the Northwest whose work compares to yours."

"A dress? So soon? But when is the wedding?"

"In a twelvemonth. No sooner than that. Lord Thomas and Lady Cecily believe we should wait if only to know our minds. I thought, perhaps, if I had the dress to look at now, it would ease the time apart and make it fly—oh, Mary! How pale you look! How thoughtless! Forgive me?"

And then Jane did something quite unexpected. She rose and embraced Mary tenderly, offering a kiss. Mary clung to her old friend and whispered: "You should never know my sorrow, Jane!"

Nodding, Jane wiped her tears and Mary's, saying, "Now then, we should talk of patterns."

ജ

THE LOOM WORKED steadily, the gentle *thud-dud, thud-dud*, comforting as Mary mechanically yet gracefully pulled heddles back and forth, beat down the warp, smoothed the fine linen with a delicate hand. Down the street, the bells of Saint Ælfgiva's struck ten o'clock. In the kitchen, Cook was finishing up for the night and singing Mozart. It made Mary laugh to hear it. Cook was another woman in Knowstone that everyone thought they knew…

Bright amber light suddenly blinded Mary; she threw hands to her eyes to shield them. Emily had yanked aside the velvet curtains and held a lamp in Mary's face.

"Mother! The light, please."

"You think to make a fool of me, don't you?" Emily growled.

"I think nothing of the sort."

"That display before Lady Isobel and Jane! You played on their sympathy and made me look a perfect fool! And the way you gaped at Erland! Lord knows what they were thinking and if they had an inkling of what you had in mind—"

"You are unfair. I wasn't gaping, and I didn't play on anyone's sympathies. I answered Lady Isobel truthfully, as is my custom to answer any question posed. Is that not what you and Father taught me?"

"You made me look a perfect fool, I tell you!"

"I swear I didn't!"

"Don't lie to me!" The words were short, clipped, and venomous. "They have every reason to hate you, despise you, and yet they love you! You're no better than a whore!"

"I am not—oh, why do you think that?"

"Well? Is there a child? Well? Answer me!"

Mary beat down the weft too vigorously and moaned when she saw the threads snap.

"Answer me!" Emily growled, taking Mary's braid in her hand and twisting it gently to get a firm hold.

"There was!" Mary snapped in a tone wrought with impatience. "Now, leave me alone!"

"Do not take that tone with me! You whore! You've made a fool of me!"

Emily yanked on the braid so that Mary screamed in pain. Mary wrenched free and blocked the hand her mother raised to strike.

"Tell me how I can make a fool of you when you do it to yourself every day?" Mary said. Her voice was even and controlled, belying the measure of her anger.

The hand came up suddenly, and Mary now saw bright blinding flashes of color, of red and yellow, as she was struck again and again with mounting viciousness. Mary tried to escape and only got as far as the passageway and thus caught she made no effort to defend herself and allowed Emily to rant, to call her filthy names and untruths, to let the blows fall where they might.

"You're no use to me!" Emily shouted as she kept administering blows. "You've ruined everything you've touched! Your husband is dead, your father's dead! You would be better dead, too!"

Emily made one last growl of disgust and left her daughter curled up on the carpet. Only when Mary heard the footsteps fade and the slam of an upstairs door did she pull herself up and sit quietly for a moment.

She didn't dare look in the mirror or touch her face. She

could feel the blood sliding down her cheek from an old wound that was freshly opened. Her face grew warm. In the morning, she would look a fright. When her heart stopped pounding and her hands steadied, Mary took her chair before the loom and resumed her work, trying her best to repair the broken threads. They would be part of the pattern; no one would notice. Nothing in life was perfect, anyway. She sang to comfort herself, one of the familiar hymns by the Wesleys. It was past six in the morning when Mary finally left the parlor and was amazed by the gray streaks of light coming through the window.

Cook was coming down to light the fires and start the day's baking when they met on the stairs. The woman gasped when she saw Emily's hatred so evident on Mary's sweet and beautiful face.

"There's nothing you can do," Mary told Cook when she began to rant about the cruelty heaped on the young woman.

"But there's a great deal you can!" the woman swore passionately. "Come, Mistress, I'll find a poultice for that welt." When Mary cried out as Cook placed a guiding hand on her shoulder, the cook swore under her breath, adding, "I'll go to market today and see to the household, Miss! We'll patch you up and put you to bed once we take care of the damage done!"

Seated before the vanity mirror in her bedroom Mary tried her best to ignore the distorted image and wondered how much of what she saw was real. She ignored the Cook's maternal clucking and sighing as she did her best to clean and salve the wounds. "I provoked her," Mary said at last.

"Why do you not listen to the whispers, Miss?" Cook moaned as she daubed Mary's face with a salve that smelled wonderfully of flowers and sage. "You can only pretend for so long."

"Do you think I cannot hear?" Mary replied. "Dear Meg, it is what everyone wants. They would be glad if I left Knowstone."

"You would be better off."

Mary grasped Cook's soft yet leathery hands and kissed them. "I know this. But where do I go? I have not enough money yet. A few weeks, months that is all I have put aside. But soon. The cathedral has ordered more linens, and I have commissions. I shall have enough, then. Besides, it is not yet time to give them satisfaction. Not before I've had my chance."

Cook's eyes grew wide, and she put a hand to her mouth. "Surely you wouldn't…!"

"It all depends," Mary whispered cryptically and then smiled.

CHAPTER 7

MARY WAS STILL sleeping.

Emily glanced skeptically at Cora before her with head bowed and repeated her question in a sharper tone. "And have you looked in upon her?" she demanded. "Perhaps she went out early, as is her custom while the weather holds?"

"No, ma'am, not since the last time I looked in upon her," Cora replied.

"Has she taken a lover?" Emily stepped closer and narrowed her eyes so that they resembled a cat's when it made ready to pounce. "You keep her secrets. You will tell me!"

Cora's head jerked upwards, and her face went white. *Aha*, Emily thought, the *girl knows something!*

Mary had an unfortunate habit of befriending those whose places were well below hers, and that independence of thought and spirit, her passion for equality in all things, made her the brunt of jokes and ridicule. This girl Cora was one of Mary's pets, and the stupid creature was emboldened by Mary's favoritism.

"So then! Who is it? Do you know? You will tell me else I'll beat it out of you, girl!"

Cora met Emily gaze for gaze and said, "As I said before, ma'am, Cook bade me bring Mistress Mary a tray, and I went in, and she was still asleep. I left the tray and came back an hour later. The tray was still there, and the food's gone cold and greasy. She is still sleeping, ma'am. It is the truth. Punish me if you must for speaking out of turn."

Emily looked the girl up and down and noted that she was steady both in gaze and deportment. The child could never lie. She was, unfortunately, telling the truth.

"Our little mouse has learned to do more than squeak now that Mistress Mary's returned! If I didn't need you so desperately, I'd turn you out with nothing but your petticoats."

"And I would deserve it, ma'am."

The comment took Emily aback, and she raised a hand to strike the girl but used it instead to smooth down her own ringlets and said, "There was a disturbance outside the park last night, some screaming. No doubt highwaymen at their practice, for the roads are dark and wild this way. I know it kept me awake. Surely my daughter, too," Emily sighed, turning away to pull on her kid gloves. They would hide the swelling and the bruises she'd given herself while giving a few to Mary last night. When she turned back to Cora to take her bonnet, she couldn't help but notice the girl's smirk. Emily struck her so hard across the face that Cora stumbled against the china cabinet and fell. The noise brought Meg the Cook into the room. Her eyes slid from Cora, picking herself up to Emily, standing over her with hands clenched as if to strike again.

"There you are!" Emily said to Cook. "When my daughter is finally awake, tell her I've gone to market, though it is a great inconvenience, and we shall have words when I return."

The mere act of grasping the latch made Emily catch her breath from the pain. She would see the doctor while in Knowstone. Better still, the apothecary; he wouldn't ask questions. He never did in the past. When Cora looked concerned and asked what was amiss, Emily waved her off with an impatient hand and hurried out to the yard where her pony and trap waited. Once secure in the vehicle, she forgot the pain her daughter caused, and by the time she arrived in the market square, the confidence in the sense of entitlement and superiority she'd nurtured and refined over the years in this dismal backwater returned. Emily glared at the boy who offered to tend the pony and trap as she disembarked and pushed past him to the apothecary's, ignored the outstretched hand expecting a penny.

Her hopes of finding sympathy and a willing audience were dashed when she entered the shop and discovered Lady Isobel and The Reverend Mr. Herrold in animated conversation with Mr. Gray, the apothecary. They were discussing roses and Mary's patterns woven into her fair cloth.

"Mistress Witherslack," Godwin Herrold said with a polite bow and tip of his hat when he saw her.

"Ah! Emily!" Lady Isobel exclaimed. "How fortunate you should come to Knowstone today. I was going to call upon you."

"Indeed? Twice in a week? How fortunate indeed," Emily tittered while examining the tinctures and unguents displayed in blue glass bottles on a shelf behind Mr. Gray. "Mister Gray," she said, "I injured my hand doing work in the gardens. Our roses are not as picturesque or accommodating as the Frankewell's, nor are they the variety Mary does so like to draw. Do you have a salve that will reduce swelling and bruising?"

"Now those roses are what we were discussing! How clever of your daughter to work them into her excellent needlework," said Isobel. "Do you know, the handkerchief she made for me was mistaken for one of the Queen's by the Countess of Exeter when she came to call? I tell you, there is no one, not one seamstress, from Chester to Bath, who can equal Mary's attention to detail and fine work."

"Indeed," Emily sighed.

"She was to come by this morning to look at the cloth for Jane's dress. She was to meet us here. Yet she did not. I hope she is not indisposed?" Lady Isobel continued.

"Perhaps she had another appointment?" Godwin suggested. "Or has gone out on her leisure? She regularly visits the bookshop. I've noticed her there time and again."

"She does have a fondness for the work of John Donne," Isobel interjected.

"For the life of me, does this village exist only for Mary Burnley? It seems that no one else is of any import!" Emily snapped impatiently and under her breath.

"Pardon, Mistress Witherslack?" Godwin asked.

Emily ignored him and gave a charming smile to Mr. Gray, the colorless man holding two vials for inspection. "I will take both—one never knows when another joust with a rose bush is the order of one's day!" she announced, and after the transaction moved towards the door and came eye to eye with Godwin.

Now here was a handsome man! Why was it that all the men who perturbed Emily were handsome as Greek Gods and possessed an inclination towards kindness? Ah, if she was as young as this curate! Was that a look of appreciation she saw in the way his eyes raked over her? The shy smile?

The poor woman; she either refused to or could not distinguish a look of contempt when it was tossed her way and assumed it was borne of passion or lust.

"I was greatly impressed with your daughter's work—the fair linens, I mean," said Godwin. "Please convey my regards to her and let her know that St. Ælfgiva's appreciates her offering."

"That is for Mister Talbot to decide, sir!" Emily said. With a curt nod of her head and a direct glare at the handsome clergyman, she left the shop.

"What do you make of that?" Lady Isobel said to Mr. Gray.

"Little," Mr. Gray said and excused himself when another customer entered the shop.

"And you, Mister Herrold?"

"I've put it out of my mind, Lady Isobel. Good day. I hope you will come to evening prayer."

"You may be sure of it!"

Out in the street, Godwin paused to watch Emily push and negotiate her way through the market and considered the episode. He did not know what to make of it or this place to which God and the Archbishop of Canterbury had sent him.

He was a stranger in Knowstone, having come only nine months before from Canterbury. Godwin was learned, liberal in thought, and surprised at finding himself in a marcher outpost after three years of service as a secretary to the Archbishop. He assumed it was a test; whether he would pass it was yet unknown. In the last month, he'd made strides: villagers were more apt to smile in greeting when he strolled through the market square, such as that afternoon, or stop to ask how he was fairing. They asked for counsel or a blessing or invited him to supper, stopping Godwin while he was on his way to an appointment. Godwin wondered if it was the fashion in Knowstone to impede those on urgent business, for it always seemed to happen at the worst time. However, that afternoon, his progress from the market to the vicarage was impeded only by a bookseller's stall. Godwin caught sight of a book he hadn't seen in months—a copy of Malory's *Le Morte de Arthur*—and paused to browse. He smiled, skimming pages once edged in gold but now tarnished, finding passages he'd loved as a boy, and came across *Sir Gawaine and the Loathly Lady*. The conversation he'd exchanged with Mary Burnley in the church after evening prayer came to mind.

What was the answer to the lady's question that broke the spell?

What a woman wanted was her own way.

Godwin snapped the book shut and put it back, only to take it up again a second later, putting down three bob for the purchase. Rather than continue on to the vicarage, he kept walking, the book tucked in a pocket, towards St. Edmund Wood. He'd seen it from a distance and heard the fantastic tales of hauntings and curious disturbances and decided he'd discover the place for himself.

When he reached the wild, wooded expanse at the edge of the village, Godwin noted was how beautiful it was. It separated a ruined abbey from Knowstone, fragments of arches and walls soaring above the oaks and towering over the wood. The afternoon sun shot rays through the trees and ruins, motes of gold dappling the ground. What used to be a cloister was now overgrown flower beds that long ago lost symmetry and function—their present use was to delight the senses. Godwin saw the timber and wattle of a manor house not far away, another half-hour's walk, and decided it must be Hazelwick.

Mary Burnley's residence, was it?

There was enough time to make a brief call, Godwin decided.

The presence of a cloaked figure in the cloister remains made him pause.

A woman was seated on a parapet with a notebook and pencil in hand. Perhaps she was sketching the landscape or recording her observations. As Godwin came closer, he saw that it was Mary Burnley. She was draped in a black shawl, her face partially obscured by the cloth.

"Hello!" Godwin greeted as he approached. "This is a happy chance, for I've been to Mister Ferryman's shop in the high street and found something quite pleasing. I have a book in which you may be interested—"

The shawl fell away as her head shot up at the sound of his voice, revealing bruising of different colors and severity, the scabs of healing skin marring the left side of her face. The look of horror on her face mirrored Godwin's, and before he could say another word, Mary fled.

CHAPTER 8

THE INCIDENT IN St. Edmund Wood haunted Godwin for days after. He forced himself not to inquire nor make an investigation, but he did go back to the wood several times in hopes of seeing her, and those attempts were unsuccessful. There was no one with whom to share this episode. No one, save Erland Frankewell.

Godwin had few friends in town. Those he thought he could befriend were in awe of him, and those he wished to befriend were totally unsuitable to his standing in society. Erland Frankewell was both unsuitable and in awe, yet well above Godwin in society. A fortnight passed, and he decided to discuss Mary Burnley with Erland.

Godwin expected to find him at The Castle and Motte that afternoon and every afternoon. At a quarter past two, he'd be knee-deep in his cups. Why was it, Godwin ruminated, as he walked down the street, that the sons of the landed gentry did nothing well but drink?

Godwin had asked that question of himself for years.

As he rounded Brides Lane from Mr. Allyne's surgery, he literally ran into Mary Burnley. He laughed in embarrassment and set her aright when their glances met. She looked away first and pulled her shawl close. This afternoon it wasn't hiding scars or bruises. Mary wore a hat that obscured most of her face.

"Good evening, Mistress Burnley! How are you?" Godwin said. The mere touch of her shoulders beneath his hands sent a pang of lust through him. Embarrassed that Mary might see how she affected him, Godwin backed away. However, as soon as he moved, he was sorry, for he wanted nothing more than to continue holding her.

"Well, thank you, Mister Herrold," she said.

He glanced up at the sky, avoiding her scrutiny, especially her lovely, clear eyes. "D'you think we've seen the last of the rain?" he blurted out.

"Not until October."

They laughed together nervously.

"Is that a new bonnet, Mistress Burnley? It's very attractive, y'know. You have a face made for hats…" Godwin stopped there, floundering.

"No. I abhor hats of any kind and wear this only to please my mother and keep her quiet. I thank you nevertheless for the compliment."

Mary knew why he stared. He'd seen her at the abbey ruins and saw the injuries. The hat was more to hide the damage her mother had done more to make her happy. She scowled when Godwin kept his intense gaze upon her.

"You haven't returned for evening prayer. I thought you might be ill," Godwin said of a sudden when she became silent and looked more interested in the grass beneath their feet than him.

"I wonder that you haven't guessed, Mister Herrold, how Mister Talbot holds me in low regard and how unwelcome he has made me feel."

"He holds you in contempt, for what reason I wish I knew."

Mary smiled and began to walk, Godwin joining her. "Don't you?" she questioned. "So you haven't heard the rumors, the gossip?"

"I've heard stories – rumors and gossip, I'm sure, but you are the guardian of your secrets."

"That's just it, Mister Herrold. I hold no secrets."

They were at the dressmaker's shop now, and Mary's gaze went involuntarily to the apricot-colored frock still displayed. Godwin noted her preoccupation and nodded, saying: "I think only you could wear such a fine thing and do it honor."

"Oh really, Mister Herrold!" she protested but smiled

shyly.

"I've made you smile!" He waited for a response, and rather than suffer delightfully and silently under her intense gaze, continued, saying: "A beautiful smile it is. It's no wonder that the women of Knowstone are so envious."

Godwin wanted to crawl away then when the smile faded. He was always saying the wrong thing to women. Was it any wonder he was still unmarried at twenty-five? Now he racked his brain for an apology. "Forgive me, Mistress Burnley! I didn't mean to be so forward."

"Good day, sir. Shall I bring the linen on Wednesday next?"

"The linen? Why yes! Yes, at five o'clock."

"Wednesday, then."

She nodded and started the climb up the hill to the castle ruins. After a moment, Godwin sprinted after her.

"I truly am sorry!" he said breathlessly.

"Your apology is accepted. Good day, sir."

"May I join you?"

"I fear I would not be good company," she said. "I go up to the castle for solitude."

"Let me be a silent, solitary companion."

"If you'd like."

They climbed the hill to the castle. Godwin followed several paces behind Mary, who scaled the wooded path as easily as a staircase. Soaring out of the hill as if it had been chiseled from it, the ruins of a Norman castle overshadowed the village and served as a milestone to travelers in the West Country heading toward Wales. As soon as they saw the castle, they knew they were in the right direction. Stopping in Knowstone for a night's rest or for refreshment was always an afterthought.

The outer curtain and bailey were gone, the stones used for buildings in the village and beyond, but the donjon and three of the twelve towers were remarkably preserved, if one overlooked the gaping hole here and there, a missing step, or part of a slate and timber roof gone. Mary paused and sat on an embrasure of what used to be a high, double-arched window. She took from the bag slung over her shoulder a little book and opened it to a particular page, and there sat reading for the better part of an hour, while Godwin silently toured the ruined hall, silently studied the profile of the beautiful young woman. When at last she closed her book, she looked up and smiled.

"You must tell me what you think," she said aloud.

What could he say? That she was like one of the beauties painted in Roman frescoes, sculpted in Greece, that he could watch the rise and fall of her breasts as she read, or walked, all day long? That he could stare forever at that one curl that fell down from her nape and dangled over her right breast and dance with every breath inhaled and exhaled, that her voice was more intoxicating than any strong ale?

"It's an ordinary castle, one built by the Conqueror or one of his vassals," Godwin said with a shrug. "It has later developments, such as the remnants of groin and barrel vaulting in places, much like a cathedral."

"You are more than theology! That is an achievement compared to other clergymen I know."

"I wanted to earn my living as an architect. My father had other plans. Fathers usually do."

"Yes," she murmured, looking down at her book.

Godwin started another tour, hands behind his back, his boots scuffing gently across flagstones intersected by moss and grass, an occasional flower that he made sure to overstep. "It's remarkable in its own way, I suppose, being here in the marches in this out-of-the-way place preserved it in a way other castles were not. So much of it still intact."

"It is extraordinary, Mister Herrold. Let me show you."

He willingly followed as she went out of the donjon to a semi-ruined building, what looked to be a chapel. Here was a solitary tomb, graced by an effigy of a beautiful woman in medieval garb. It was undefiled and looked as if someone had tended the grounds and kept vagrants and animals away.

Godwin tentatively put a hand out to touch the carved folds of the lady's gown to run his fingers along the name on the sepulcher. "Ælfgyva. An Anglo-Saxon name. The patroness of our parish church, I think?"

"Yes. It means 'elf gift.' "

"A beautiful name for a beautiful woman. No doubt she was the chatelaine."

"It was said she was a witch for her powers of healing."

"Do you believe that?" Godwin laughed but not unkindly.

"No. What people do not understand they blame on the devil and other evils in the world. This lady was poorly used by those she thought loved her. She was my ancestor—and she was the Christian wife to the lord of the region, the *thegn* before the Normans came and built this castle. Before they took her."

He looked at the face of the effigy, to Mary's face, in surprise.

"This knowledge has only just come to light. Justin—my husband—found the records in his research of local antiquities. She is my mother's family. Her man, a thegn called Wulfnoth, was killed in the battle at Hastings. His land and property, his fortune were taken by The Conqueror, who gave all to one of his vassals. But the greatest prize was Lady Ælfgyva, who was of royal blood from the house of Wessex–a kinswoman of Alfred the Great, descended from Cerdic. She and Wulfnoth's hand-fast wife tried to escape when the Normans came. The other woman was used and died of her injuries. Ælfgyva showed remarkable strength and heroism as she fled. It is said she could not be forced no matter how many men tried to take her. She fought with sword and ax, with bow and arrow, and lived in the wild. Finally, she was captured and kept a prisoner here, raped and used when the Norman lord threatened to burn the village, kill the men and children and rape the women if she did not give herself up in their places. And so she became a bed slave. The people in the village accused her of complicity with the Normans and killed her. She was made a saint for the goodness and piety no one saw in her, for they never looked past the beauty of her face and only saw what they wanted, what the priests and bishops told them to see. Just before her death, there was one knight, an Englishman, who was the beneficiary of her goodness. She found him outside the castle walls and took him in despite the threat to her safety. He'd been wounded in a rebellion against the castle lord. Her knowledge of healing arts saved the knight. It made no difference. The local priest declared her a witch for the power she held over men and cursed her and every generation after. And then she burned."

"What power had she?"

A foolish question, he thought now as she gazed at him. *The power of beauty. Of sexual attraction.*

Mary picked some wildflowers and placed them on the effigy's hands. After a lingering gaze, she smiled and walked back the way they came. Once again, Godwin was in her wake.

"Mistress Burnley!" Godwin said when he caught her up. "Mistress Burnley, is this why you are held in contempt and scorned by the villagers? This ancient history?"

"Only one of many reasons, sir," she replied with a sad smile.

"It makes no sense."

"If someone wishes to find fault, they will, or they will dig about to find something and use it. Or spin it out of cobwebs or the air, and soon it takes a life of its own."

"May I do anything for you? To assist you in this difficult time?"

"The difficult time is past, at least, the worst of it is. Thank you, Mister Herrold, for your concern."

"Should you require anything, you need only call at Saint Ælfgiva's."

Mary shook her head in disagreement and smiled. "No. Unless it is on a Wednesday evening. I'll take my leave now. Good day."

He watched as she passed down Whitecastle Street towards St. Edmund Wood, wondering what it was that made her so grave and distrustful. He was preoccupied with the mystery of Mary Burnley and the story of Ælfgyva as he went into The Castle and Motte in search of Erland Frankewell. Here was another mystery he hoped his friend could solve.

CHAPTER 9

GODWIN SETTLED INTO his usual booth in his usual corner, taking a book of John Donne's poetry from a pocket.

"Have you seen Erland Frankewell?" he asked Dorcas when she brought a tankard and pot of ale.

"He's come just now, sir," Dorcas answered, nodding at the man entering the common room. "Shepherd's pie and broth, some bread, and cheese?"

"Please," Godwin answered as he hailed over Erland. "And another tankard."

Dorcas smiled and got out of the way of Erland's hand trying to grab her bottom as he slid into the booth, but couldn't escape the sloppy kiss offered.

"Ah, Dorcas, if you were a lady," Erland chuckled when he succeeded in kissing her again.

"That's just it, sir. I am. Put your tongue back in your mouth and let me get Father Godwin's supper!"

"A hundred pardons, milady! I have been reprimanded," Erland said. When she was gone, he turned to the man smiling at him across the table. "Mister Herrold. How are you this evening? You look...perturbed. I'm sorry if my lovemaking ruined your plans. Did you want to tumble her?"

Erland's eyes were uncommonly bright that evening; for once he was still sober, and here it was a quarter past eight.

"It's not that kind of hunger. I've had nothing to eat all day. One of the pitfalls of bachelorhood, Erland. No one to remind me to eat or prepare the meal, and I've no desire to stay in nights with the Talbots."

Dorcas returned with the food and slammed the second tankard on the table before Erland, throwing him a warning look as his hands started to roam.

"Have you dined?" Godwin invited him.

"I wouldn't call that dinner such as it is, but yes, I have."

Godwin shrugged and began to eat, turning a page in the book of poetry that now caught Erland's educated eye.

"Donne? His sermons, or his poetry? Hunh! Poetry. The reading of it will only make you sweat for a woman."

"Don't think I haven't once or twice. What's on your mind, Erland?"

"What makes a man choose the priesthood?"

"You're not chosen. It's given to you. You're born to it, and it's damned difficult trying to ignore it. Is that all you've come to talk about?"

Erland took meat and bread off of Godwin's plate, folded them together, and bit in. "There are things. But for the moment, your problem seems greater than mine."

This response prompted Godwin to pour a tankard full of ale and slide it towards Erland. "In wine, there is truth—the same for ale, I think," he hinted. "I've nothing to complain about."

Erland took a drink and studied Godwin carefully. "I don't understand why a man as handsome as you and with money to inherit would settle for the priesthood."

"Did I not explain that?" Godwin laughed.

"You did, but then, holy orders may hide a multitude of secrets and sins."

"For some. Not for me."

"No, I don't suppose so. Not for you. Now for myself, if I was in holy orders,"

"Who is she?" Godwin wanted to know as he dug into his meal.

"Maeve Pinkerton. The bitch says the child she carries is mine."

"Is it?" Godwin asked, not missing a bite.

"It might be, or it might not. Besides, I'm in love with another girl. Mistress Witherslack's daughter."

Godwin paused and then continued eating. He poured ale for himself and drank quickly and deeply. "Yes, I've met her," he said.

"What do you think of her?"

"I think that Mistress Burnley is a very unhappy woman. And this is none of my business."

"Don't let it be said I was the cause of her unhappiness!"

"I wouldn't know."

"What do you think of her?"

"I've already told you."

"In so many words, you didn't."

"What I think should be of no concern to you."

"If you could see your face! You're dying to know the truth about her," Erland laughed.

"As much as you're dying to tell me," Godwin said, smiling. "Tell me then, so I can finish my meal, such as it is, in peace."

Erland relaxed. "We were engaged to be married. My parents thought it unsuitable at first to marry the only child and daughter of a penniless vicar but thought better of it when they met Mary. Such wisdom, beauty, such compassion in one person was not to be believed. Her father, The Reverend Mister Witherslack, was against the marriage. My father is a Roman Catholic. Mister Witherslack died after a fall from his horse, and we thought perhaps our way was clear, Mary's and mine. And then there was the problem of her mother. Emily Witherslack inherited her late husband's debts and compounded the embarrassment by acting as if nothing had happened and she lived above her means and station."

"Embarrassment?"

"It is rumored she took a lover not long before her husband died. The extravagant living, the debts, it was too much. We were separated, Mary and I. I went away to Germany to complete my education, and Mary climbed into bed with a history professor from Oxford!"

"You don't know that. I've met her, and it seems unlikely

that a woman of such seriousness and grace as Mary Burnley would do…something like that," Godwin scoffed.

"Seriousness and grace? No one thinks of seriousness and grace when Mary Burnley comes to mind. You've seen her. If Botticelli were alive, he'd paint her."

"Put it behind you and get on with your life. Find another girl to your liking."

Erland's face suddenly took on a new passion, a new hatred. He leaned forward and whispered: "You don't know Mary Burnley. With Mary, nothing is simple! Wait until you've been with her for more than an hour and then consider how you feel, how different everything will be after that, and how different the world will look! It's not that simple! After one look, you'll wonder what it would be like to lie in her bed, to feel her against your manhood, to kiss that mouth, and join your bodies as one. There's not a man in Knowstone who doesn't! I had that taken from me!"

"She is a widow now and free to marry. Your mother holds her in high regard. I've heard her praise of Mistress Burnley. What's to stop you?"

"Maeve Pinkerton."

"How strange that a man so in love with a woman as you profess to be would allow anything to keep you from her bed."

And since the woman was Mary Burnley…

"The lady herself prevents me. She is in love."

"Well," Godwin said, downing the rest of the ale in his tankard, "you're not likely to take her by force. This isn't the twelfth century."

Was she in love?

"No matter the black stories whispered about me, I am not a raper. She is in love, and any man hoping to possess her as a lover or wife has no hope," Erland growled. "Damn him!"

Does he curse me, I wonder? Godwin thought.

"She's in love with a ghost. Her husband, Justin Burnley!"

❧

GODWIN LAY ON his back and stared at the ceiling, studying

the patterns of broken plaster and water stains, listening to the drone of the April rain. The clock in Talbot's study chimed *one . . . two . . . three . . . four . . . five*. Godwin burrowed into his pillows deeper and deeper still, but sleep would not come. He ruminated over pastoral calls he'd make after morning prayer, the text for his sermon, taking baskets of food and clothes to Bottle Street. Still, thoughts of Mary disturbed the orderly list of daily matters and became erotic fantasies and not for the first time. He saw her dressed in a gown made of diaphanous linen, saw how every curve and sinew of her body was made known and watched in his mind's eye how he stripped her naked between their hot kisses and they lay together in a castle bedchamber in a different time and world…

Godwin cried out for the woman he wanted in his bed, whose face and form were shadows in his monastic bedroom of the vicarage, and spilled his seed.

He rose violently and cleaned up, then threw on his clothes, went out, and found himself on the path leading into the wood. To the east, he could see the pale orange ribbon of the sunrise not far away.

Birds escaped from the trees as Godwin kept on the path, the lowing of cattle and sheep bleating in nearby pastures answering. He didn't know how tired or cold he was until he saw the park and chimneys of Hazelwick.

Slowing as he approached the hedgerows that served as fencing, Godwin stared at the third storey windows, spotting honey-colored light in one. The silhouette of a woman reflected on the curtains, and he waited breathlessly, hoping.

No, it was a servant.

Godwin had every intention of going back to the vicarage when he spun about and found himself face to face with Mary Burnley.

"Mister Herrold!" she exclaimed, genuinely surprised to see him. "That you are so far afield from the village—is it my mother? Were you called?"

"Your mother?" Godwin stammered. "Oh no. No! I

couldn't sleep, and so I found myself wandering through the wood and came upon this house."

"You've found my home," Mary commented as she slipped past him to unlatch and go through a gate further down the path. She turned and smiled. "How strange that we should both find ourselves restless, Mister Herrold."

"Pardon?" Godwin was distracted by the perfection of her eyes and mouth; the eyes uncommonly bright for so early in the day, the lips rosy and tempting.

"I, too, could not sleep." She lingered there at the gate, alternately watching the horizon and, if Godwin's assessment was close to the truth, him. "I cannot understand why of late it has been such a trial to fall to sleep," Mary continued.

For myself, I know why! Godwin mused silently. He looked over at her and offered a shy smile. "I often think that there are times when we are visited by our hopes and fears late at night and that it is for a purpose. God requires from us only our unconditional love and acceptance of what has been ordained for us, according to those gifts bestowed at our births. We are given this quiet time, the most silent time of day, to ponder what we must do."

Mary's face brightened, and she nodded thoughtfully. "Of course. I have been pondering my future here."

"And what have you divined?"

She watched the flight of two sparrows as they soared and dove between the branches of sycamore and yew trees and lit together, chirruping as the sun started to glow in the wood. "There is nowhere I belong, sir," she said quietly, sadly.

Godwin leaned over the gate and raised her lowered chin with a finger so that he could see her eyes and the perfection of her face. Close enough to kiss. He smiled, a tender offering, when she met his gaze.

"What if I managed to find a place for both of us?"

The bells of St. Ælfgiva's rent the morning silence. Both looked in the direction of the alto chime. "It's Sunday morning!" Mary remarked as if startled by the fact.

"Unfortunately, I must go," Godwin replied but took no steps.

"Is it so onerous a duty, your calling?"

"At times, such as today."

"But it's Sunday, sir!" Mary laughed.

"I would rather spend the time with you."

Mary lowered her face so that he couldn't see her blush or smile. "And I you," she said quietly, "but you may not. Ah! You look so sad! I have it: I'll join you at church. Perhaps I will shock the good people of Knowstone, I swear there's no doubt of that!" she laughed again. "I'll come to show my support for your ministry. Ah, how the bells ring! You must be on your way, sir."

Unfortunately for me, Godwin thought as he smiled, nodded, and started back, then wheeled about. "Mary!" he called and was relieved when she returned to the gate, lips slighted parted as if ready to question. Lips he longed to kiss. "Will you meet me by the stream in the wood? After church, three o'clock?" When she looked at him quizzically, he added, "To continue our conversation, of course. You and I seem to be outcasts— lodgers in a greenwood hell."

"How perceptive of you, Mister Herrold." A moment passed, and she nodded. "I should be glad to keep your company this afternoon."

"By the stream. I'll look for you."

"And I for you. Good morning, sir."

"Good morning, Mary."

Godwin went back the way he came, looking behind him only once, and was glad for it. She was smiling and waving.

so

"...FOR IN THE night in which he was betrayed, he took bread, and when he had given thanks, he brake it, and gave it to his disciples, saying, 'Take, eat, this is my Body which is given for you. Do this in remembrance of me."

Godwin elevated the Host, and in doing so, was distracted by a sudden disturbance in the nave. As his back was to the congregation, he couldn't see what was happening and glanced nervously at Talbot standing to his left, his expression worried.

"The Burnley woman's come to church!" Talbot hissed.

Rather than maintain their reverence, the congregation turned and whispered, nudged, and gawped. Mary Burnley took a seat in the back near the door. The usher nodded politely in her direction and took a few cautious steps away.

The church was crowded and uncommonly warm for this, his first Eucharist celebrated at St. Ælgyfva's; no doubt that was the reason for the press of curious people in a nave usually sparse with worshippers. Godwin felt sweat on his forehead and dabbed it gently with a handkerchief after his reverence to the transubstantiated bread.

"Likewise, after supper, he took the cup, and when he had given thanks, he gave to them, saying, Drink ye all of this, for this is my Blood of the New Testament, which is shed for you, and for many, for the remissions of sins. Do this, as oft as ye shall drink it, in remembrance of me."

The chalice quaked as Godwin elevated it and set it again on the altar. Talbot frowned as Godwin consecrated the bread and wine, gave the invitation to Communion, especially when Mary Burnley knelt at the rails and when Godwin approached with the consecrated bread.

"The Body of our Lord Jesus Christ, which was given for thee, preserve thy body and soul unto everlasting life. Take and eat this in remembrance that Christ died for thee, and feed on Him in thy heart by faith, with thanksgiving."

His hands trembled as he brought the bread to Mary's mouth and felt the warmth of her breath on his hand. Their eyes met, and Godwin saw a hint of a smile on her lips. In his mind, he saw them together in bed, sharing the divine moment, sweet words and sweeter kisses exchanged…

Godwin dropped the consecrated bread, the Body of Christ, and watched, horrified, as it fell to the sanctuary steps. An urchin snatched it up, midst scandalous gasps. His wails echoed through the church as his mother dragged him out, threatening her retribution and not God's. Afterward, Godwin avoided the stares and whispers when the service was over, but he couldn't dodge Talbot's wrath. He was putting away his vestments in the sacristy when Talbot entered and thumped the Bible on a cabinet top.

"Caught the Miller boy trying to take the Bible," Talbot groused. "One wonders if he thought he'd get two and seven for it in the market! Miserable brat! His father brings home enough to feed them."

"Everyone knows it's the property of St. Ælfgiva's," Godwin muttered, smoothing the wrinkles out of his cassock before hanging it up. "A shilling a week for carting wood doesn't buy bread, milk, and ale for six children and a wife."

"The poor we shall always have with us, yes, yes, I know. How would we preach if we've no scripture to read from? That's what I want to know!"

"Go out and preach the Gospel, and if we must, use words?" Godwin quipped. When Talbot frowned deeper, added, "Saint Francis?"

"And forget the sins, I suppose? Forget their own lack of discipline and morals, leading less than godly lives? Blaming their poverty on God?"

Godwin ignored the look and the comment, saying, "Intolerably warm today—I think I'll go for a ride if you have no need of me after I make the rounds."

"I have no need of you whatsoever!" hissed Talbot.

"I'm sorry! It's been a while since I celebrated the Eucharist. I was never placed on the *rota* while at the cathedral—"

"And why should you? Priests are aplenty in the cathedral. Archbishop's lap dog! Now I suppose you'll close your eyes and ears to the smirks and sniggers. You were doing well enough until that slut entered the church!"

Godwin frowned as he pulled on his coat and tried to push past the man but was held back. "It was an honest mistake, borne of inexperience. And you do the lady disservice by calling names," Godwin muttered.

"If you're going to be seen in public with her and champion the girl so shamelessly, you'd do well to encourage her to leave this place once and for all and go with her. She's not wanted here!"

"Neither am I."

Talbot said nothing to that, for he'd no desire to see the satisfaction in Godwin's smile if he disagreed. Talbot knew who was unwanted and unnecessary.

Godwin retrieved the baskets from under the table in the sacristy and then opened a hamper beside the door, taking out clothes and bundles of food. His favorite task of the day was going to Bottle Street, the poor neighborhood of Knowstone, and distributing alms, hearing the woodsmen and laborers' stories. There he was received for who he was: a man who listened, a man who cared. He wasn't given long, disapproving glances for what many considered failures.

Mrs. Teamer pulled him inside for a cup of tea. She was a weathered woman of indeterminate years whose beauty was still reflected in her grass-green eyes and the dimpled smile that showed teeth. The hair bound up in a cap was streaked with gray, but golden strands stood out. Godwin was led into a shabby but neat parlor where two fair-haired girls were busy at their needlework, and a little boy struggled with a psalter, lisping the verses of Psalm 139 from a gap in his teeth. The children came to their feet when they saw their visitor.

"Now, children! Here's Mister Herrold come with the bread and apples," Mrs. Teamer announced.

"Sara and Polly," Godwin greeted as the girls bobbed in curtsies. "Michael, you improve every day. Soon we shall have you preaching, eh?" The girls giggled at this, and little Michael threw them a hateful glance, muttering about silly girls.

"I wanted a word, Reverend," Mrs. Teamer said low and waited until the children were settled again before pouring two cups of tea and sitting at the table across from where she'd put Godwin. She pushed a cup towards him and smiled, nodding.

"It's about Michael. Perhaps you know that Mister Talbot has offered to pay for Michael's schooling in Halton?"

"The parish has a discretionary fund to pay for the education of those who cannot afford the cost," Godwin answered.

"But Halton, sir? Charnel House School?" Mrs. Teamer whispered, and when Godwin gestured that he did not understand, she continued: "It is the lowest of workhouses! The school is but a disguise. The boys are made to work in the churchyards, and there is an arrangement between the headmaster and Mister Talbot. And, God forgive me for saying this, but Mistress Wright's boy was used for other purposes. Money was paid so that he might dress in a girl's frock for the amusement of the headmaster! I dare not imagine that happening to my Michael!"

Godwin ruminated on what the other purposes would be and nodded slowly. "What may I do for you, Mistress Teamer?"

"Speak with Mister Talbot, sir! I do not want my boy going to Halton. I would never have agreed to put him in school if Mister Talbot hadn't been so insistent. Three pounds isn't worth it!"

"We shall have words. I will bring you my report on Tuesday next."

"Thank you, sir!"

Tea enjoyed, and the conversation moving on to more pleasant topics, Godwin said farewell for the day and made a promise to come to Sunday dinner next week. It was time to move on and the other families in the street. He was appalled to hear other similar tales.

He would have to do something.

The bells of St. Ælfgiva's rang two o'clock when Godwin returned home. He had another appointment and one that would surely be more pleasant, one that he'd looked forward to all day. He took his horse from the stables and rode out towards St. Edmund Wood, glad to be free if only for a short while from the claustrophobia and darkness of Knowstone.

There was a stream deep in St. Edmund Wood, far back from the road into Wales. Godwin had found it some months before when he'd gotten lost on one of his first adventures. A clearing where the stream cut through the wood, an oasis, became a sanctuary in troubled times. He always found it easier to pray and confess his sins in such a place, find solace in creation when humanity was left wanting.

Godwin drew up rein when he saw Mary seated on a blanket with a picnic supper spread before her. A shawl was cast aside, and she'd let down her hair. A book was open in her lap, but she seemed to be interested in something at the stream, and his approach was unnoticed until the horse whinnied.

"Mister Herrold! You're early!"

"Am I?" he asked, dismounting. "I thought I was unpardonably late. And you've brought tea!"

"I could not resist. I had Cook put up a basket, and what do you think? She is more curious about my afternoon than a cat who espies a mouse-hole in the wainscoting," Mary laughed. She extended a hand towards the picnic. "Please."

He fell on his knees at the edge of the blanket and watched as she poured two cups of tea, offering one and then holding the other, waiting until he drank before she did. They dined in silence for a long while, enjoying one another's company and the idyll around them. "I don't remember when I've had a more pleasant day and company," Godwin spoke up.

"I think if you searched back into your memories, you'd find a day or two, surely?" Mary asked as she handed him the biscuit tin.

"Not particularly. I am expected to be sober and all seriousness and forsake pastimes. I should never be the country squire."

Mary studied his appearance, noting the plain white shirt and trousers, the riding boots. He looked like a country squire, a look worn easily. "More's the pity, Mister Herrold, for if you were a country squire, you would be unlike your peers. Your tenants would have good cottages and livings if what I've heard about your work in Bottle Street is any indication of the truth."

Godwin now came round and sat beside her on the bank. He began tossing pebbles into the stream, watching the rings wander out and disappear one by one, how the water turned to glass and reflected the clouds in the sky, and became still as it reflected sunlight on Mary's beautiful face. "I do what I must because there is little I can do," he said.

"Have you so little regard for yourself? Mister Herrold, some would think otherwise. Your kindness and generosity to the neighbors in Bottle Street are known throughout the village."

"Time will tell. Nevertheless, it's not my duty to judge. There's too much of this world I know little of."

"Ah, you've gone from the schoolhouse to cloister."

"It's readily apparent?"

"But nothing to be ashamed of."

"And neither have you anything to be ashamed of."

"Do you know me, then?"

"I was told you fell in love with a gentleman of means, but you were forced apart, and you found another man. It happens. Other than your excellent charge of needle and loom, that is all."

"Oh no, it's more than that."

"You needn't tell me."

"Your office gives you leave to listen."

"Mistress Burnley, if you please, this is not the confessional."

"My name is Mary."

She was looking at him now. It was in a friendly way, but Godwin felt much as he had the night before and the night before that. Would this longing and dread not go away?

Mary reached down to gather the flowers that had fallen from her basket, and Godwin noted the graceful curve of her neck and shoulders escaping from the *décolleté*, the round, high breasts barely hidden by her frock.

This lady was not meant for widowhood…

She smiled up at him, and he said, "Say what you will. Mary."

"I was engaged to be married to a local gentleman, Erland Frankewell, but my father disapproved, and we were separated. Then Justin Burnley, a professor of history at Oxford, came to Knowstone on his way to Wales. He was writing a history of the Northwest and stayed a while to undertake research. We met by accident at the book shop. He was beautiful, and I was in love instantly. He was penniless out of youthful frivolity: he'd been to Paris and kept the company of the worst kind, from artists to whores. But he was good of spirit and heart, and soul, and he proposed marriage after our acquaintance grew to mutual love, and I accepted."

"And did you marry of your own free will?"

"Of course! He would not have it otherwise, but my mother objected to the marriage from the first. She had hoped for a reconciliation with the Frankewells. A knight's son was better coin than a penniless scholar. There were rumors, too, that my mother and Justin . . . I never ever believed them. And so, when our pleas and arguments fell on deaf ears, I went with Justin in secret to Warrington, where we were married. But when we returned…" Her voice faded, and Godwin thought he heard a painful sigh. "I was called a whore by my mother and Mister Talbot. It was assumed we married in secret because Justin had taken my maidenhead and got me with child. Mister Talbot preached sermons on how the Whore of Babylon was amid Knowstone. There was more whispering and conjecture, more unkind talk. And so we left. We went to Oxford and lived happily there. And then, for Christmas, we went to London."

Her voice trailed off, and Godwin marked the tears starting to wet her lashes and glisten on her cheeks. "Mary, don't trouble yourself."

"We went to London. Christmas last he wanted to surprise me and took me to the opera. When we returned to our rooms in Westminster, he took a sudden illness and died on Christmas Day. And now you know more than anyone."

"That you should share this with me,"

"Don't wonder. You're the only person in Knowstone who doesn't condemn me to a circle in hell for what I did."

"This illness. Was Mister Burnley an elder man and in poor health?"

"He was twenty-six. The youngest Professor of History at Oxford. He was Saint Sebastian. His beauty I shall never forget. Michelangelo surely thought of my Justin when he sculpted his David. I thank God that his illness did not ravage him as it might others—no one can account for his illness. I cannot."

Godwin dared to ask: "Do you love him still?"

"I shall always love him. One doesn't stop loving. Only the love changes. And you find that love in others and in other aspects of your life."

"Would you, will you ever consider love again?"

"Of course." Their eyes met, and Godwin did not dare ask or expect more. The answer satisfied him. They sat quietly now, making daisy chains together. Suddenly Mary spoke up. "I've grown used to being alone, Mister Herrold, but I'm not altogether used to the poor treatment I receive at the hands of others."

"Why do you not challenge your critics? Let them know what they believe is a lie?"

"I am a woman, and it would be considered unwomanly to face my accusers. I shall have my vengeance by success in my endeavors. You see, Mister Herrold, I am going back to Oxford to the University. I will apply for coursework. Ladies are allowed to attend lectures. I have decided that."

"I applaud your nerve!"

"Do you think it is nerve? Were I a man, it would be the next logical step in my improvement."

Godwin felt the hot color of embarrassment and being in the wrong flood into his neck and cheeks. "What I meant to say, Mary, was that for a woman of your accomplishments and beauty,"

"Mister Herrold, now you sound like all the rest. I shall prove all of you wrong! Justin's beauty was no hindrance to his achievements, and surely yours was of no moment or importance when you entered the seminary. Why should one of the requirements for a lady to achieve be that she is plain or, God forbid, ugly?"

"Do you think me handsome?" Godwin asked, feeling quite pleased.

A hunter's horn shattered the pastoral silence, and Mary immediately got to her feet, dusting her frock of leaves and gathering her things. Beyond the clearing, riders were evident, and she saw that they were men of Knowstone.

"Oh, dear!" Mary sighed.

"Don't leave,"

"You'd best be off, Mister Herrold," she warned; "Another black mark against my reputation would be nothing, but you have a living to make. It would be a terrible thing to have your reputation compromised."

"What others think of me means little. You are gentle and kind, and if Knowstone knew your sorrow, they would humbly beg your pardon for so many slights and unkind behavior."

"But they do, and they don't care. Mister Herrold, how can you, knowing these people, believe otherwise? Now go."

The riders were closer and within sight.

"Permit me then…"

Godwin nervously and hesitantly took Mary by the shoulders and left a lingering kiss on the sweetly scented skin of her brow, another gentle kiss, chaste and sweet, on her lips. He was relieved when she returned the favor with a smile and touched his face gently rather than pull away or strike him. Godwin swung easily into the saddle and, bending down, brought Mary to him with an arm about her waist. They kissed again, a more passionate and telling display of affection. This was done in full view of Martin Frankewell and John Merrow, out with their hunting party that afternoon. As they approached, Godwin bade them a good afternoon very cordially and rode off, giving his courtesy to Mary with a tender smile, a kiss on her palm.

Let them think what they would.

CHAPTER 10

MARY ARRIVED HOME from her afternoon in the wood just as a storm broke, a thunderstorm that lasted for most of the night and brought with it two days of blustering rain and winds. She was locked up at Hazelwick with her mother, who was no more pleased by the weather's foul turn than Mary. The long hours were filled with the familiar routine at the loom, reading and reliving the afternoon by the stream.

"What is so amusing?" Emily demanded of Mary when she came into the far parlor and found her daughter smiling while she pushed the heddles back and forth.

"Life!" Mary answered.

"Pah!" Emily said and boxed her daughter's ear. Mary paid no attention to the smarting or the ringing. To her, it was the sun shining down on the brook and glistening off the water; the ringing was the sound of the birds in the wood. Cora and Cook saw to it by service and presence that the tenuous peace held and all breathed easier when by Wednesday morning the skies cleared, and Mary was able to go out.

The path through St. Edmund Wood was barred by a tree that had fallen in the storm. Mary glanced about and frowned, looking for another way to the village. She shifted the basket of linens and set it on the trunk. Lifting her skirts, she tried to step over it, but it was too broad and slippery. Her attempt brought her tumbling into bracken and mud.

Mary picked up her things and hurried, glancing at the sky. It would be five o'clock soon, and it was Wednesday.

It was no use. She'd have to walk through the abbey.

And the ancient gate was open.

Mary thought she was the only person who knew about

the gate and knew this shortcut into Knowstone. As she approached the Virgin's tabernacle, Charles Talbot came around the ruins of a pillar. Mary shrieked, her cry setting the birds to flight.

"What do you want?" she demanded.

"Anyone can walk here, Mistress Burnley. I'm on the way to the church. I took a walk through the wood, as in the days of your father. Do you remember?"

"Do you believe in faery folk, child? Come, let me show you a place that's full of magic…"

Her father's voice in her mind was carried off by the wind picking up.

"Those days are long ago, sir. I have to go. I have an appointment in Knowstone."

"Mustn't keep the vicar waiting, Mistress Burnley. Mustn't break another man's heart!" Talbot rasped and grabbed her hand to prevent her from leaving.

"Let go of me, sir!"

"He is your knight errant, then? Your champion?"

"What do you mean?"

"Did you tell your tale of woe? The poor, unfortunate widow misunderstood by family and villagers?"

"If I said anything, it would be the truth."

"An intelligent man, a man of the world, wouldn't believe a word of it. Godwin Herrold is neither, but then, there isn't a word from your sweet lips he would doubt!" Talbot pulled her closer. Trembling more in anger than fear, Mary struck him across the face. Talbot merely laughed and whispered, "'Your daughters play the whore, and your daughters-in-law commit adultery!'"

Mary hadn't heard that paraphrase of scripture for years, and she went cold at the sound of it. "Sir, I tell you now, unloose your hand or suffer the consequences!" she said, trying to keep her breath and voice even and void of all emotion.

"There's no one who would believe you! Why don't you leave? Throw yourself from the castle ruins? There's no place for you except the fires of hell!"

"I said, let me go!" Mary growled and felt her hand and arm go numb from the painful grip he had. "And let he who is without sin cast stones, Mister Talbot!" she said as she managed to free herself and run toward the village.

"No one wants you here!" Talbot shouted after her. "No one will ever believe you!"

No one paid attention to the girl running up Whitecastle Street, nor did they care that she was weeping, her dress torn and spattered with mud. She paused only a moment to drop her basket of linens at the door of the church.

℘

AT HAZELWICK, EMILY found herself once more at a disadvantage, having said good day to Mr. Talbot only an hour ago and now to find herself with another guest and her daughter not yet returned from the village. Would the stars never align for her? Would Mary always embarrass her thus?

Emily tried her best not to stare at the young man sitting in her parlor. His coat and boots were the finest she'd seen, and the way his hair fell rakishly over his brow gave Erland Frankewell the look of an artist or poet from London society. Thank goodness she'd thought to wear her best gown that afternoon!

"And your mother, is she well, sir?" Emily simpered, pouring out another cup of tea."

"But you saw her yesterday, I think?" Erland said.

"Yes, that is true—I do fondly remember when she condescended to pay a visit here at Hazelwick. And Jane. Now there's a handsome and obedient girl!"

"Lady Isobel will be glad of your concern." Erland glanced at his pocket watch and then at the door. "You said she'd be home by now, Mistress Witherslack?"

"I am sorry that Sir Martin will not condescend to you and consider your wellbeing and your happiness. We were all hoping for a spring wedding in the new year. Now it seems it will be your sister Jane and not yourself."

"Mistress Witherslack, I cannot stay for much longer. Please convey my greetings to your daughter."

He rose to leave, but Emily all but pushed him back into the chair. "You know how the path from Knowstone can be treacherous after a storm. I expect Mary will return at any moment. Please."

"Very well."

Emily sighed and then offered a pretty smile. "Just think, this formality would all be forgotten if matters had fallen into place as they should have if Mary hadn't taken it into her head to play the damosel in distress."

"Mistress Witherslack, I implore you, if all you wish to do is revisit a painful episode, you do your daughter and me a great disservice. I must be on the way. Will you tell Mary that my business with her is urgent, and perhaps she will receive me in the morning?"

"My daughter is disconsolate. Her husband's death makes her grief extraordinary and compels her to do things against her nature. I wish only to secure a comfortable future for her, and who better than the gentleman who first loved her?"

"As to that, I cannot say. I do not know if she would be willing."

"Are you saying that you would reconsider?" Emily asked hopefully, sitting up straighter in her invalid's chair and removing her shawl.

"I say nothing, Mistress Witherslack."

"Oh. I see."

The front door closed, and Mary's voice in conversation with Cora silenced them. Emily glanced hopefully towards the parlor door, and her face lost all of its color when Mary entered. Erland was on his feet though his face was flushed, the coloring that comes with seeing a beloved no matter how he or she looked.

Dress soaked and filthy, torn where she had fallen, her hair in lank ropes about her neck, scratches on her face; this was how Mary presented herself.

"What have you done now, Mary?" Emily moaned. "Cora!" she shouted. "Cora! Where is that slovenly maid—ah! There you are, girl. Draw a bath for your Mistress. Mister Frankewell, I'm sure she will be more presentable after a bath and dry clothes. If you would wait just a while longer?"

"I cannot, but," Erland's heart was pounding at the sight of her, the sweat rising on his palms, and the longing he'd felt for so many months returned. He swallowed to relieve a dry throat and then said, "Mistress Burnley—Mary, I came to speak with you about a business transaction,"

"Ah! Is that what the fashionable are calling it these days!" laughed Emily.

"I would speak to you alone," Erland replied. "That is, with your servant present. I would not wish to compromise you in any way."

"Erland, you may join us in the kitchen. I'm sure the impropriety of watching a young woman wash her face would not compromise you in any way," Mary jibed as she wiped her nose on her sleeve. "It's this way, if you don't remember."

In the kitchen, Erland seemed more relaxed and watched in fascination as the maid helped Mary salve cuts and bruises on her face and hands from her fall, washing the dirt away gently. The pretty maid blushed and begged his pardon while she put up a screen and from behind it changed Mary's ruined dress for a nightgown and robe.

"I meant to come by," Erland said, his back to the screen.

"And so you have."

"There is talk, Mary."

"Oh, dear!" The voice was amused and sarcastic. "When is there not in a place as small and inconsequential as Knowstone?"

"Have you taken Godwin Herrold as a lover?"

"No!" Mary came around the screen in her robe and gown, and Erland lost his train of thought while he stared.

"My father saw you in St. Edmund Wood."

"Has no one in this place anything better to do with their

time than gossip? You know me, Erland."

"You were seen with the curate alone in the wood. You were seen in an embrace."

"And why should that offend anyone? I may be a widow, but I have not taken a vow of perpetual obedience to my dead lord and master," Mary said. "I have no obligation to you any longer, nor to any man."

"Is he your lover?"

"No. I tell you this plainly. And I tell you despite it being none of your business or the concern of anyone else in Knowstone. What I do is of no importance to anyone save God. For shame, Erland! And here I thought you knew me to my soul!"

Erland looked as if he studied the pattern of tiles on the floor while he fumbled for something in his pocket, drawing a small box from it—a jeweler's case containing a ring.

"That is the problem, Mary. I do know you well and hope now that you would accept this."

The case was offered, but Mary only frowned and stepped away as if it contained the most lethal of poisons.

"I wonder at your foolishness, Erland! Your father has said time and again that you must not renew your suit, or you would find yourself penniless and without a home, without means to live! I have heard this threat more than I care to, especially since I am the cause of his unreasonable anger!"

"You mistake my meaning," Erland said. "It is the wedding ring I purchased three years ago. I ask you to take this and leave Knowstone. Sell the ring—it would be a year's living at least. Get away from here. You deserve better."

"Out of sight, out of mind?" Mary hissed. "No."

"Send her away," Erland demanded, jerking his head toward Cora, and once she was gone, Erland took Mary in his arms and kissed her and was not at all surprised by her indifference.

"If you will not leave, then be my mistress. My lover! Our fate would be tolerable if we had something to share, and I could look forward to every moment we could be together. I'll put you up at the lodge. Do you remember the place? It's mine to do what I wish, and nothing would please me more than to make it your home. Our home! We would be happy there, together. You could be away from your bitch of a mother."

"You would make of me what is whispered and rumored, and all of it untrue," Mary responded quietly.

"I would not!"

"You would! I have no desire to be kept and petted, hidden away from the sight of others, or standing quietly at the back of a parlor to exchange glances and love tokens while you have a wife or another mistress on your arm and no one says a word about your behavior!"

"I care only for you, Mary! I love you! I have always loved you!" Erland proclaimed, leaning in for another kiss, but was prevented by Mary's hand against mouth.

"And yet you would not speak up for me in that dark time and instead went away to hide."

"Can we not forgive one another?"

"We?" Mary now shoved herself out of his arms and stepped back. "I have done nothing that requires your absolution or that of anyone else!"

"Come with me! Let's leave together! We can go to Paris, or—"

"—you must go, Erland."

Mary led the way through to the hallway and was met by Emily, whose face was bright with expectation as the couple moved quietly to the door. "So? Is it decided?" she asked, looking from one to the other. Mary ignored her and opened the door for Erland, who looked at neither lady as he came forward.

"It is. Good day to you, ladies," Erland barely whispered on his way out.

The door closed slowly, quietly.

Mary now looked at Emily and said, "It is not what you would wish for."

"What have you done?" Emily hissed, following after her. "What did you say to him? What did you tell him?"

"Only that his attention is undeserved and unwanted."

Emily let out a scream of anguish as if her heart had been ripped out of her chest. The howl made Cook burn herself on the stove and set Cora to wailing when she dropped some of the best china while setting the dinner table.

"You're no good to anyone, least of all me!" Emily shrieked. "Everything you've ever done, everything done for you, has come to nothing! You're ungrateful! You're selfish! Any girl in Cheshire would give her life to marry someone like Erland Frankewell! You're willing to give up a comfortable life, good society, and for what? Principles! Education!"

"These are attributes for which men are admired. Why not women? Do you think I would ever be happy as mistress of a great household?"

"But it means nothing that you make yourself a burden on mine!"

"I shall leave," Mary spoke up, and that stopped Emily's hysteria for a moment.

"What? What say you?"

"Oh, Mother, don't pretend to not have heard me," Mary sighed on her way to the dining room to help Cora.

"Where will you go? The stories that will be told,"

The door was closed quietly on Emily, and Mary went around the dining table to where Cora sat sobbing before the shards of a porcelain teapot. "Dear Cora! Let's see what can be done here. I'm afraid she'll take the cost of mending this old thing from your wage packet," Mary said as she knelt to help salvage what they could.

"I'm sorry, Miss! I thought she'd murdered you!"

"I'm very much alive, Cora."

At dawn the next day, Cora helped Mary pack her belongings and carry them to a cottage at the end of Bottle Street. They left quietly and before anyone was awake. A note was left for Cook, who went about her chores holding back tears but felt a sense of independence and victory at Mary's boldness.

Godwin learned of this and could not believe what he heard from Mrs. Teamer on Sunday when he arrived to take dinner with her.

"Just as the sun came up, there was Mistress Burnley with a cart and a maid! She took old Mistress Cuthbert's place, the one we call Street End Cottage, the large place with the yard and garden, the barn!"

"I'd not seen her all week," Godwin murmured, and when he noticed Mrs. Teamer's smile, added, "She comes on Wednesdays with the linens."

"Make no mistake, Mister Herrold, we all think kindly of Mistress Burnley and welcome her. We'll look after her. Now! Here's a fine turnip stew and some eggs, fresh bread and butter, and some apples from the woodlanders. It's not what you're used to, but it's good fare."

Godwin offered a blessing and tucked into the hearty meal. As soon as dinner was scraped and sopped up from the plates and the ale pitcher drained, he thanked Mrs. Teamer for the fellowship and hospitality and finished his rounds of Bottle Street, his last stop at Street End Cottage.

Cora answered his knock and immediately stared down at the alms basket. Before he could get a word in, she said, "That should go to someone truly in need." When Godwin stared in puzzlement, Cora added, "Begging your pardon, Reverend, it's what's in the alms basket. My mistress sewed the clothes and knit the socks. She'd be distressed if you thought she was in need of them. We lack for nothing, truly."

"Is your mistress about?" Godwin ventured.

"I'm sorry, sir, she is working on Lady Jane's wedding linens and won't be disturbed."

"Please convey my greetings?"

"I will, sir."

With a nod, Godwin said good afternoon and went home. Walking away, he heard the sound of Mary's loom keeping cadence with the song she sang.

The week dragged on until Sunday arrived again, and Godwin saw that he wore his cleanest shirt and a new collar, his boots polished. Rather than walk, Godwin took the horse, for perhaps Mary would entertain the thought of a ride to the wood. Again he made the rounds in Bottle Street and ended at Mary's cottage. It was Mary who answered his knock this time.

"Mister Herrold, is there something you wanted? Is my mother ill?" Mary asked, a tinge of curiosity in her voice, rather than concern, given the query.

"Your mother—? Oh no, no. I've finished my rounds today and wondered if you might come on a ride to the wood."

Mary glanced around Godwin at the horse nibbling on the dried grass in front of the cottage. "Forgive me. Had I known you would come to call, I would have arranged my day accordingly. This afternoon I must go to Saltfield to bring samples of linen to Jane."

"Then perhaps another time?"

"Yes," Mary said, again eyeing the horse that was now sampling her roses. "Until next week? We can walk up to the castle if you'd like."

"The castle it shall be. Good day, Mistress Burnley."

Another week passed, and it happened that when Godwin arrived at Street End Cottage, Mary had decided to wait at St. Ælfgiva's. Godwin wheeled about and ran back to the church, ignoring the jests and calls from the Bottle Street neighbors, didn't see John Merrow and Sir Martin Frankewell watching with raised brows as he raced through Knowstone. He found Mary sitting on the ruins of a low wall under one of the great oak trees near the porch. She stood and curtseyed in greeting.

"Mistress . . . Burnley!" Godwin sputtered from his exertion.

"Oh dear, I think you have already taken the greater part of our exercise today!" Mary said, trying not to smile at his eagerness. "The fulfillment of your obligations does you great credit, Mister Herrold."

"I must . . . I should apologize! I should have made myself clear as to where we would meet! Well, shall we on?"

Mary smiled and took the arm offered. By the time they were on the path to the castle ruins, Godwin's heart had stopped racing from his sprint and now raced from being in Mary's presence. They scaled the hill and the staircase to the bailey, pausing a moment to admire the greenwood and in the distance the misty purple hills of Gwynedd.

"How could you forsake such beauty?" Godwin murmured, taking in the magnificent view.

"Pardon?" Mary asked, her own thought interrupted.

"I beg your pardon, Mistress Burnley, for disturbing your thoughts."

"You may call me Mary, Mister Herrold," she said, smiling.

"Mary, then. And you must call me Godwin."

"It is easy to forsake all this," and here Mary gestured gracefully with a hand towards Knowstone, "when there is so much ugliness hidden beneath the gaud. Surely you have seen it?"

Godwin nodded, ducking his head so that she wouldn't see the flush of embarrassing color over his face. "When I heard that you quarreled with your mother and that you had moved to Bottle Street of all places—"

"Of all places?" Mary exclaimed. "Bottle Street is a street like any other, and it has its merits! The tenants are not so full of self-importance and have no lack of compassion or consideration. Because their pockets are not lined with pound notes nor heavy with coin makes them no less important to God!"

"A wondrous homily, Mistress Burnley. I have offended you. Again, I must beg your pardon," Godwin confessed. "I am forever caught up by my tongue and assumption. Is it any wonder the Archbishop sent me here?" This last was spoken in almost a whisper. Mary had seated herself on what used to be a stone bench built into a wall of the donjon and glanced up.

"I did wonder," she said. "Would someone choose to come to a place like Knowstone if he had other choices or opportunities?" Now she met him, eye to eye. "Is this your desert wilderness? Is this your Gethsemane?"

Godwin shrugged and sat next to her. "Where but a place like this is there a greater need for the Word of God and the blessing of Christ's example? You asked me once if I believed what I prayed and preached. Yes, though the belief comes from struggle and much difficulty."

"Grace shines through you, Godwin," she almost whispered, offering another beautiful smile.

"Only because," he paused and shook his head.

"What, sir?"

"Because of the brightness of your own grace."

Expecting a modest blush or a downcast gaze, Godwin was surprised by the unwavering hold she kept with her eyes. The bright crystal color reflected the sky and showed no coquetry or shyness. There shone through was an independence of spirit and thought—a kindred spirit there with the purest of longing. Not a base carnal desire, but something otherworldly, and he cupped her chin in his palm and kissed her without hesitation.

"I am yours!" Godwin whispered into her flower-scented hair, "I am yours with all my heart, my soul, my body. I am yours!"

Mary put a hand to his lips, which he kissed as she said, "Godwin, do not be so easy with your promises."

"No promise, but the truth."

"I have been given assurances and see where I have been led by my belief in them."

Godwin stood and held out a hand. "Will you walk with me?" When she hesitated, "I see I must prove myself to you. Neither my words nor presence should give you cause to fear or be distrustful. Allow me to plead my case?"

She rose after a moment's hesitation and placed her hand

in his. The grasp was warm and secure, strong. Godwin led her down to the village, and they parted at Bottle Street, where after a kiss and embrace, they made plans to meet on the morrow for another afternoon walk. Again, Mary waited for him at the church. That day she wore a new dress of pale pink muslin and carried a shawl of celery green with embroidery in rose-colored silk. A braid of ribbons in the same colorways held back her hair. However, Godwin first noticed the brightness and warmth of her smile that rose to her eyes.

Godwin suggested a walk to the stream in St. Edmund Wood, which pleased Mary until he led her towards the abbey, and at the gate, they paused in conversation and in their walk. He noticed Mary's reluctance to go forward and swung the gate closed again, leaning upon the post.

"A beautiful place, this," Godwin said, smiling down at her.

"I played here as a girl."

"Not so long ago, I should think!"

"There is the queen's throne." Mary pointed to the ruins of the chapter house where the abbot's stone bench still stood against a wall's remains. "I spent many afternoons hiding and playing there," she reminisced aloud, a hint of wistfulness in her voice. "I did not have poppets to play with as other girls in the village, so I brought my books and gave them names. Shakespeare was Jane, the Prayer Book was Patience, the Bible was Anna. I would arrange them around the throne and offer royal decrees. They were my ladies in waiting." Now Mary laughed softly and put a hand to her cheek, looking away. "Ah, you must think me strange!"

Godwin gently turned her face towards him and was glad that she smiled but was surprised by the tears in her eyes. "Would Your Grace have time in your appointment book for an audience with a poor priest?" He gestured past the gate and could see how Mary tensed as he slowly pushed at the gate. Godwin waited until she finally nodded, and he drew her into the abbey precincts.

The sound of their boots scuffing across the autumn leaves and bracken, the wind rustling the trees, were the only sounds as they approached the chapter house. Once there, Godwin led Mary to the 'throne' and ceremoniously placed her and offered a courtly bow. They both laughed, and Mary laughed even more when Godwin picked three large stones from the ground, and kneeling, put them before her, saying, "The ladies Jane, Patience, and Anna, Your Grace! They wait upon you as the poor priest begs a favor of the Queen of Hearts."

"What does the good Reverend require of his Queen?" Mary laughed softly, extending her hand for a kiss.

"My lady, all that I require is your acceptance of my love, for I do love you."

The playful moment turned serious when Mary leaned forward and bestowed a kiss on Godwin's brow. She held his face in her hands and studied its beauty, remembering every line, mark, and color, for her sleep that night. "Godwin, I will grant this petition, but you must take it as a promise. Give me time to think."

"As much as you desire," he said hopefully.

Mary kissed him gently, and he drew her into his arms, and there they embraced in the ruined abbey with the late afternoon sun spilling ribbons of light through the trees and columns of stone.

They walked to Bottle Street arm in arm as sweethearts are wont to do and whispered endearments as Godwin strode off, leaving with a promise to call on the morrow and looking back more than once.

"He's a kind and thoughtful man," Cora commented as she stood with Mary on the doorstep and watched him go. "Why he should come to a place like this…"

"To do some good, I think," Mary answered. "Shall we have supper?"

There was no ceremony in Street End Cottage. Mary and Cora shared their duties and meals; Cora's position was more of a companion and sister than service. The only parting of the ways came when supper was done, and Mary went out to the barn where she kept the loom and worked well into the night while Cora looked to all things domestic. And so it was that evening, in the midst of a familiar, comfortable routine, when all things took a turn.

CHAPTER II

THE PATTERN WAS coming along nicely. Mary's fingers traced the roses centered on the hem of the pure white linen and damped down the heddle for several more rows, weaving bobbins back and forth until the top of the flowers showed, and the border was done on another tablecloth for Jane's trousseau. A good day's work! She rose to retrieve another spool of linen thread and to stretch her back. Now, where were those shears? When she stood, a small stone fell from a pocket. Mary rescued it from the shed floor and smiled. 'Queen's Gold,' Godwin called it and pressed it with a kiss into her palm after retrieving it from the forest floor growing in the abbey ruins. It wasn't a pebble but a shard of blue window glass worn smooth from years of exposure to the elements.

A blue the color of Godwin's eyes.

How could life suddenly find so much brightness, she wondered, after so much misery? There was so much to be thankful for, and Mary was sure it was God's will that brought it about.

"Those are pretty flowers," Cora remarked, nodding at the flowers Mary put in a pottery jug as the table was set that evening.

"We found them in the chapter house in the abbey ruins," Mary said as she lovingly arranged the blue bells.

Cora paused as she folded a napkin. "The abbey? But I thought,"

"A true goodness is there," Mary replied, and she kissed the maid on the cheek.

Supper was laid, and after a quick prayer of thanksgiving, they shared portions of rabbit stew, barley porridge, and apples and cheese. Conversation traveled from the new dress Cora made to the tea set found in the market to Mary's plan to open a shop in Chester.

"When I've finished Jane's wedding trousseau, I will have enough money to find a house and shop. I have money set by— Justin was poor, but he left me something," Mary chatted. "You'll come with me, I hope?"

"And Cook? I saw Meg yesterday, and she's miserable if she's anything, M'am," Cora replied hopefully.

"Meg! We should have taken her with us. Perhaps it's not too late. Tomorrow, you will deliver a letter to my mother asking for Meg. If need be, I'll pay her the wages Mother owes and settle that account so that she may come free and clear."

"Oh, Mistress! I am that glad!" Cora said.

Mary was serving up the evening's surprise—a lemon cake—when someone knocked. Cora looked at Mary quizzically. The second and third raps were more insistent than the last. "Someone may need help, Cora. See who it is," Mary instructed and wiped her hands on her apron, waiting.

"Sir!" Mary heard Cora exclaim, and the maid returned with Erland.

"No welcome for a friend?" he demanded after seconds of silence passed. Mary only glared.

"The hour is late, Erland. You shouldn't be here."

"I've come for the necklace that is rightfully mine. My mother's diamond pendant."

Without taking her eyes from him, Mary drew up the necklace from between her breasts and tugged at the chain until it broke. She held it aloft, saying, " Lady Isobel bade me keep it as a token of her friendship with me, not mine with you. But take it."

The necklace was shoved into Erland's pocket. He leered at her and came further into the room, looking about as if searching for something or someone. "I also came to bring you news of a friend's passing. I know you haven't many friends in Knowstone. This death will be particularly cruel."

Her pulse was hammering in her ears, a cold sweat broke out on her skin, which, despite the shivering that overtook Mary, burned. "Who—?" she asked, swallowing hard. She knew; just by looking at Erland's flushed cheeks and lopsided smile, she knew.

Please, God!

"That pathetic curate from Canterbury. The Reverend Godwin Herrold. He deserved it, and I was glad to do it."

"You'll burn in Hell!" Cora hissed. "Never was a kinder man come to Knowstone! Not since Mister Burnley! You'll burn in Hell!"

Erland was still smirking, waiting, as Cora broke into sobs and then finally ran out of the room. Mary pressed against the edge of the table for support while trying to make sense of his news. "You are damned for all time," she whispered. "He was nothing but a friend to you. You are evil, heartless! That you would come here and proudly confess such a crime,"

He threw himself down into a chair and started to howl with laughter. "You just proved me right and won me three crowns. I knew it!" Erland said as he helped himself to the cake and poured a cup of tea.

"What are you saying?"

"I've been saying all along to John Merrow and others that the curate is besotted in love with you and you with him. That he would be your next conquest before the next moon if you haven't bedded him already."

"Then you didn't—?"

"Of course I didn't, Mary! D'you take me for a murderer? I was having a lark at your expense."

Mary crossed to the door and threw it open. "Get out! You can be cruel when clear-headed, but worse, if not evil, when drunk. Go. I never want to see you again. Do not speak to me, do not even greet me in the market!"

"It was only a bit of fun, Mary!"

"Go, I said!"

Erland moved in for a kiss, but Mary pushed him out the

door and barred it shut. She shoved a trembling hand into her apron pocket and clutched at the pebble, rolling it over and over between her sweating fingers until she was calm.

"Oh dearest, he's a monster!" Mary said as she found Cora hiding in the kitchen and embraced the distraught girl. "What a cruel, evil joke that was! He's not dead," she whispered, rocking her gently. "He's not."

"Truly, Miss?" Cora asked, wiping her eyes.

"We'll go to church in the morning, and you'll see for yourself. Go to bed. I'll do the washing up. I have more work to do tonight."

It was past midnight when Mary finished the dishes, swept the floors, and then locked up and went to the barn. She had an idea for an embroidery design for Jane's nightgowns and shifts and happily sat at the desk set up across from the loom and started to draw ancient vines and patterns like those from the times of the Danelaw and the Anglo Saxons. They weren't fashionable but mysterious, evocative, and would look wonderful on the neckline and hems of underpinnings and shirts. Mary blushed as she drew. Something to start a conversation. She imagined wearing the shift while having a conversation with Godwin. The fabric would be the softest lawn, perhaps a nainsook, and the drape would skim lightly over her body with the vines and love knots dancing across the hems and *décolleté*...

The pounding on the door startled Mary, and with lamp in hand, moved towards it slowly, listening. The pounding became more violent, insistent when she didn't respond. Mary saw her shears on the loom bench, slipped them into her pocket, and then carefully and slowly unlatched the door.

Erland shoved past her into the barn, and Mary backed away as he came slowly forward, offering his arms for an embrace, a drunken grin screwing up his mouth. He lunged and caught her before she could escape, nuzzling her face and neck like an excited puppy, his hands wandering inside her dress until she violently pushed him away, and he stumbled against the desk.

"Still playing Virgin of the Greenwood, Mary?" he laughed. "Why don't we settle our differences man to wife?"

"We're not man and wife."

"Aren't we? Didn't we pledge ourselves before the vicar at Templeton?"

"You're a fool to think that a childhood promise would be legally binding. Get up and leave. Leave me alone."

"God forbid I should disturb your idyll here in Elysium!" he mocked. "When I suggested that you leave Knowstone, I did not mean to the poorest neighborhood in the village. If you insist on staying, at least have enough regard for your mother to live in a better place."

"It's no business of yours where I live. How strange that you should come to call and champion my mother!"

"She made me see reason if you must know."

"How is that possible?"

"If you moved to Saltfield, that would be enough regard."

"As your mistress?"

"As my wife. Make good on our promise and marry me— no! Wait before you speak. You know that had circumstances not been so…contrary to our desires, you would be wife to the heir of the Frankewell estate and a great lady in your own right."

"Do you think that is my chief desire, Erland? To be ornamental? To suffer through interminable afternoon teas and social calls, to wait at half-past three of an afternoon to receive callers and talk about, what? The latest fashions from London? The polish on the young lord's boots? What her ladyship whispered to his lordship at dinner and how it scandalized court? Your opinion of my worth as a wife is very low!" Mary snapped.

"You're mistaken. I hold you in very high regard, Mary."

"Is that why you mocked and ridiculed me before other men with that insidious wager?"

"Jealousy. It is jealousy and longing. You are the most

beautiful and desirable woman in the county, and we, I, do not know why you waste it on strangers like Burnley and now Herrold."

"Does your good friend Mister Herrold know how you feel?"

"Mary, I did not mean,"

"You made it very clear what you meant! I see it would be advantageous to you and the men of Knowstone if I were to set myself up in a bothy like Mistress Quayle on The Riding. At least then the rumors and speculation of my being a whore would have some truth in their ground."

"And you know, you of all people know, what I have sacrificed to make good your name and reputation!"

"I did not ask you for those sacrifices."

"I am giving up my inheritance. I am forsaking my family," Erland started, rising to his feet. Mary stepped back and away, fingering the shears in her pocket. "I've done things, Mary."

"We have nothing to say to one another, Erland. You'd better go. In times past it was a pleasure to have your company. I cannot say the same now."

"Hear me out, I beg of you—"

"No! We've nothing more to say!"

"Haven't you wondered about the illness that took Mister Burnley? It was sudden, wasn't it?"

"How would you know—?"

"Don't you remember? I was in London at the time."

A chill overtook Mary as her memory was jogged. *They met Erland by accident…*

"Was it a cordial he drank or a poison when you dined at The Margrave?"

It happened so quickly that Mary would later think it a dream.

Erland seized Mary, smothering her with a kiss and tearing at her clothing. He pushed her up against a wall and pinned her against him while he tried to force himself in her, and he was almost successful when the shears came out of her pocket and sliced his perfect face down the cheek, a scarlet ribbon from the brow to the jaw line.

"Whore! Bitch!" Erland screamed. When he lunged for Mary again, she raised the shears, but Erland knocked them from her hand. Mary grabbed a vase of flowers and hurled it at his head. The force of the blow made him stagger, and he found his way to the door, yowling, "You'll suffer for this! You'll die, Mary! I hope you rot in hell!"

Doors opened and closed along Bottle Street as Erland found his horse and made it gallop east to his father's estate. Mary ignored the curious neighbors' stares as they peered out from windows and doorways, bolting the door quietly. For a moment, she stood trembling, breathing deeply and summoning calm. Then she glanced down and saw the blood-stained shears, throwing them down where they clattered under the loom. The metallic ring echoed through the barn.

Chapter 12

"Rot in hell, Mary Burnley! Damn you!" Erland screamed into the woods as his horse went down after jumping a fallen tree, and he was pitched into the darkness. He rolled out of the path of the wounded horse and lay on his back for a few minutes, getting his bearing, listening to the ragged breath of the dying animal. He had no knife nor gun to put it out of its pain, so Erland staggered to stand and looked about for a weapon, finding a rock, which he used to crush the animal's head. Erland minded not so much the loss of his favorite roan but the walk to Saltfield that gave his thoughts leave to pierce his drunkenness.

His boots crushed the dried autumn grass carpeting the ground in places and made the sound 'Mary' as he walked eastward toward the cluster of lights that was his father's Tudor manor. His valet put down his glass of whiskey and jumped to his feet when Erland entered the house through the servants' quarters and came into the hall.

"My Lord—!"

"My horse fell in the wood near Hazelwick. Have a bath drawn and give me some of that," Erland growled as he reached for the man's glass. "Everyone else abed?"

"Yes, sir."

"Good."

"Are you hurt? Shall I call for Doctor Allyne? I'll send a man to get your horse."

"The horse is dead, and I won't need a doctor. Just a bath."

"At least a bandage and ointment,"

"A bath. That's all."

While the valet saw to the bath, Erland washed the wound on his face and did his best to staunch the bleeding. Fortunately, the shears had done little except graze the skin, but the wound was starting to burn, and his head pounded from too much liquor and the fall. Still, another drink would dull all the kinds of pain he felt now. Once he settled into the steaming and fragrant bath water, Erland relaxed and was drifting off to sleep when he heard the door open and the soft clip of slippers on the carpet.

"Sir? I heard you come in, and your man told me of an accident in the wood."

Maeve Pinkerton looked severe in her black livery, prim hands folded one on the other at her small waist, a waist ringed round by a fine leather belt from which hung keys. She was a beautiful woman with the fine features of a porcelain sculpture, pale skin, and red lips that would be more desirable and enticing if she smiled.

"Where is Lady Isobel?"

"Asleep, sir."

"Lock the door and come here." When she did as ordered, Erland pointed to the cake of soap and the sponge. "I don't need to ask, do I?"

Maeve knelt and dipped the soap and sponge into the water and stropped the soap across the sponge until a thick, creamy lather was worked up, and she applied it with careful hands to his back, kneading gently.

"That's not what I meant!" Erland hissed. "I don't need to ask."

She came around and rubbed the sponge across his neck and shoulders, down the breastbone, and to his stomach. Erland's hand guided hers to where he wanted it, and he arched back in the water as she drew the sponge back and forth until he groaned and then suddenly yanked her into the bath, laughed, and then kissed her hard.

Removing her soddened clothes was difficult, but Maeve made no attempt at modesty, for she knew it would anger him.

She'd seen these moods before, and drink always made it worse. Erland unpinned the heavy gold hair she wore round her head like a halo until it fell past her hips in thick waves that caught the light and spread out like golden threads on the water. Maeve's shining, smooth and wet skin excited him so that he grabbed hungrily at her and knelt over her in the bath, sloshing water everywhere. Afraid that he would push her down into the water for one of his perverse games, she was ready to protest when he brought her to her knees and kissed her again. One arm went around her hips. With the opposite hand, he stroked and kissed her breasts and neck. "You're not her. You're not Mary, are you? You won't play cruel games and torment me? You'll let me love you?" Erland whispered between kisses.

"If you'd like, I can be your Mary. Mary as you'd have her. We can make believe we're in the abbey where you kissed her first. The grass is soft like a swan's down in a feather bed," Maeve whispered and closed her eyes as the kisses became bites. The caresses were bruising and angry. She eased back and wrapped herself around Erland, feeling desire mount as he began to move rhythmically with every caress that was urgent and demanding. "Mary is calling you her dear, sweet, love…she lies back on the ground, her hair barely covering those high, proud breasts that you long for every time you see her, her shapely legs and small waist, the curve of her hips fit with yours."

It was Mary clutching him; Mary was clutching and gasping as they moved as one until the senses were indistinguishable but acute, tantalizing, and powerful.

&

"THERE'S TUPPENCE IF you want it."

Maeve ignored the gesture of payment for her service, and seeing that her bright gold hair was once again in its prim halo, she wrapped Erland's bed robe around her and bade him a good night. She would be of service again tomorrow night if he so desired. Someone would come, too, to take away the bath and mop up the floor. She left him seated at his desk and wrapped in a dressing gown. He paid no attention as she left, and he continued to read what he'd just penned.

Downstairs the clock rang three in the morning. Erland stared over at the fire. What more could be said? He turned back to the letter. Now the words came easily, and by dawn, he had said all. The letter was sealed and placed on the silver tray for the butler to find.

"It's better this way!" he said as he applied the hunting knife to his wrist and watched as the drops of blood multiplied and fell to the antique Turkish carpet.

No one noticed his absence at breakfast. Lady Isobel and Sir Martin were used to their son's escapades and errant ways. He was a lazy son of nobility, wasn't he? Bored. Waiting for the old man to die so he might inherit the wealth. Martin often commented that he looked back on his own misspent youth and wondered how he survived.

"Perhaps he spent the night in Knowstone. You know how he drinks to excess and plays cards at The Castle and Motte," Martin said reassuringly to Isobel, but the screams of one of the maids brought him to his feet and upstairs where he found the servants gathered outside Erland's bedroom. They parted and scattered when Martin barked at them to go back to work. He nearly swooned when he saw his son's pale, ashen body slumped over the desk, the pool of blood surrounding the chair and trickling towards the door. Martin controlled the urge to wretch for only a moment and would have emptied his guts there in the hall had he not been face to face with Maeve and The Footman. He was the master of the household and must be strong.

"Do not let your mistress come near this room!" Martin cried hoarsely, trying to contain his emotion. He turned to The Footman and shouted, "Find Wells and tell him to send for the doctor and the constable and be quick about it! Pinkerton! Do not enter that room!"

Maeve ignored the order and went in, showing a pretense

of restoring calm and order, and knelt at the chair, touching Erland's cold, lifeless face, mindless of the blood and the metallic, rancid stench.

"You foolish boy!" she whispered while brushing back his hair. "How can this be? Only yesterday evening, we made love again and again, and you swore you'd love me for all eternity, that you'd care for our child!" She caught herself when she noticed one of the parlor maids peeking around the door. She looked about carefully, hoping to find nothing that would implicate her in this tragedy or reveal anything of the liaison, and saw the diamond necklace in Erland's hand and scooped it into a pocket when no one was looking. After a moment's hesitation, she took the letter and handed it to one of the trembling maids. "The master will want this. Bring it to him straight away."

Hours later, Maeve approached Martin while he sat in his study.

"How is his mother?" Martin inquired, his voice slurred by fatigue and wine.

"The doctor has given her a sleeping draught," Maeve replied, standing quietly before him with prim hands at her waist. "Is there anything you require, my lord?"

"The housekeeper has seen to everything?"

"Everything, my lord."

"Her ladyship will have need of you, then."

"Yes, my lord."

Martin sat quietly for a moment and noticed she was still there, looking up with eyes swollen by grief and tears. He held the letter in his hands.

"How simpler it would have been to let him marry the Witherslack girl! This could have been prevented," he sobbed then.

"Oh my Lord, I think not!" Maeve crooned, kneeling before him. "Mary Burnley despised him."

Martin glanced at her, puzzled. "Is this true? But I thought…"

She nodded slowly, the words coming easily. "They quarreled yesterday, Mary and Erland—openly in Knowstone, on Whitecastle Street. Mister Herrold is paying court to her, and when Master Erland wanted an explanation of her conduct, they quarreled violently. Begging your pardon, my lord, it is all very odd indeed. It is a curious event when all's said and done."

"Are you saying that Mary Burnley—?"

"Who am I to say? She plays as if she's as timid as a mouse or seems to be so. But old habits die hard, don't they?" Maeve took from her pocket the necklace Erland had taken from Mary in their quarrel and handed it to him. "You must know, sir, that she came to beg his forgiveness yesterday evening. I saw her here, in his rooms."

Martin took a moment to comprehend the implication of Maeve's words and the look in her eyes. He shook his head and muttered, "Impossible, not her!" as he stormed out of the room. Maeve glanced down at the necklace he'd dropped and studied the workmanship, the cool brightness of the diamond pendant.

"God and His saints, forgive me the lies I've just told!" she whispered, "but someone always has to pay, Mary Burnley!"

Chapter 13

Mary ignored the stares and whispers as she waited her turn to leave the church. She sat in the back of the nave against the wall, in a corner, where she had hoped to be inconspicuous. Now she took Cora's hand and gently pulled her towards the narthex where Godwin and Mr. Talbot stood, greeting worshippers.

"Did I not say he was well, Cora?" Mary whispered. "Erland Frankewell says the most unkind things."

"Where are the Frankewells?" Cora asked, looking around. Mary glanced at the empty closed box pew set apart from the rest, the expensive one, close to the altar. Every Sunday it was packed with family members and servants.

"Perhaps they've stayed at Saltfield this morning. They have a chapel."

It occurred to Mary that she wasn't the only person who noticed the Frankewells' absence. Others in the church were discussing the family in the same hushed tones.

"Good morning, Mistress Burnley," Godwin said.

"Mary," Mr. Talbot sniffed.

"The choice of Bach this morning was divinely inspired," Mary complimented Talbot, who ignored her and hailed John Merrow. Seeing her discomfort, Godwin said, "The music was a gift of Isobel Frankewell."

"The tune is one that she is fond of," Mary replied, ignoring the hand Godwin extended in greeting. "Wachet auf, ruft uns die Stimme. Have you heard the entire cantata, sir?"

"Yes, and I had hoped to speak with Lady Isobel about the choir singing the cantata at Easter this year. How odd not to see the family this morning."

Chattering over music and keeping a discreet distance was not how Godwin had hoped to greet Mary that day, surprised as he was to see her in church and with her trembling little maid. Still, if it kept Mary in the narthex a while longer...

"Whatever can be the matter that Lord and Lady Frankewell did not come to church today, especially when you went to the trouble with the music, Mister Herrold!" spoke up Katherine Merrow as she pushed her way past Mary and Cora.

There was something wrong, and Mary wondered if it had something to do with Erland's visit the night before. As if reading her thoughts, Cora suddenly blurted out, "I don't know why Master Erland would say that he killed Mister Herrold, do you, Mistress?"

"What?" Godwin asked. Everyone around them grew silent and waited.

"It was a poor joke. Erland was deep in his cups last night and came to call. I sent him away. Good day, Mister Herrold. Mister Talbot."

Mary dropped a coin in the poor box and left with Cora trailing her, asking if she'd said anything wrong.

You said more than enough, Mary thought as she hurried away without courtesy or another word.

The absence of the Frankewells was still on Mary's mind that afternoon. She'd given Cora the day off and would have enjoyed the solitude and quiet had it not been for her encounter in the church. For certain, the events of yesterday evening had troubled last night's sleep, and she almost didn't leave the cottage that morning but for her curiosity to know the truth. Knowing Erland had played a cruel trick and Godwin was indeed alive made her get out of bed and go to church. Courage was a gift that showed itself at the worst of times, and Mary was grateful for that, but it fled when there was a rap on the door. Fearful it might be Erland, she took a knife and slipped it into her pocket. If he tried anything again, she would finish the job and take the consequences. To be free of such an evil man would be worth the punishment of death.

But it was Godwin, who carried a basket and a bouquet of flowers, and smiled brightly when she finally peeked out.

"Godwin—Mister Herrold!" Mary said and threw the door wide.

"I thought you'd appreciate a gift," Godwin said as he set down the basket and removed the linen covering several books. "I hope you don't mind," Godwin murmured, taking her trembling hand and kissing the palm. "I am a persistent suitor."

"And you woo me with poetry," Mary teased softly. "Come, have supper with me."

A meal of cold fowl, fruit, cheese, and ale Mary brewed was set, and they enjoyed this *agape* while discussing their respective days, not knowing of the drama being played out at Saltfield. Godwin helped with the washing up, and when Mary reached to put cups on a shelf, he drew her into an embrace and gave her a lingering kiss.

"This is natural and right," he whispered huskily in her ear. "I have no care for what the people in this village think or say. I only care for you and for us, for we shall be together!"

His words made her heart leap, and she wanted nothing more than to stay in his arms. For the longest time, they clung to one another, and finally, she led him to the settee by the hearth, where she picked up her embroidery and patted the space beside her. Godwin sat and picked up one of her books, and while he read, Mary was at her needlework. The only sounds were the homey noises from the street and the cadence of the mantle clock keeping time.

This is how it should be. This is what will be. This is meant to be, the clock ticked.

"Will you read?" Mary asked as she rose and selected one of the books in the basket, bringing it to him. She snuggled in Godwin's arms as he read selected sonnets of Shakespeare and John Donne.

"Your choice of poetry is bold, Sir!" Mary laughed.

"Bolder than I could ever be. I wanted these words to

describe the joy, the delight I feel," Godwin said and leaned forward. "And my lips,"

They kissed, and one kiss became many and with gentle embraces that were long and intimate until Godwin pushed himself away, saying, "I want you too much, and if I stay any longer, we both know how the afternoon will end," he said breathlessly.

"Then you must go," she whispered teasingly as she planted kisses on his forehead, cheeks, and lips. "And leave me to sweet rest and sweeter dreams. At least in my dreams, I'll have you in my bed."

"You'll have me then?" His eyes were bright, animated, full of joy.

"Have I not made it apparent, sir?"

"Then I'll come back this evening, and we'll make plans," Godwin said after a last kiss. She watched him stride away, his gait quick and lively, and ignored the frowns and stares that strangely came her way from the neighbors.

✆

NO ONE AT The Castle and Motte said a word to Godwin when he came in for supper. Erland was suspiciously absent, and Godwin thought nothing of it until he asked Dorcas, and she began to weep.

"Is Erland away?" he asked innocently.

"Didn't y'know, Father? Haven't you heard? Erland Frankewell killed himself yester night."

The news stunned Godwin, as it should have. Immediately he mouthed a prayer. "Why did no one tell me? I should go to Saltfield—" he said.

"Begging your pardon, Father, they might not want you there."

"I was his friend! I am his friend!"

"That's as may be, but they do blame you."

Godwin threw two shillings on the table and hurried home where Charles Talbot was just as cryptic as Dorcas when confronted.

"Sometimes, Godwin, I feel I am a father looking after his errant son," Talbot sighed, putting away his letters and folding his hands neatly on the desktop.

"I'm not to be looked after like a spoiled child or heir, sir."

"Of which you are both!"

"One, but not the other, and not my fault entirely. Have I done something wrong, sir?"

"Perhaps you should tell me! Since you arrived in Knowstone, you have gone out of your way to show your disapproval of provincial spirituality and to remind us that you had a better place in Canterbury!"

"Never have I done that! Why do you hate me?"

"I hate you for what you are: a son of privilege who is given a place in the Church of England only because his father has an income large enough to bestow a chantry! A man who is given an appointment with the Archbishop of Canterbury only to keep him quiet and out of trouble! And when he abuses these privileges and appointments, he is sent away to a provincial parish to be hidden from sight!"

"I can't deny what you've said. It's the truth. But tell me why I am blamed for Erland's suicide."

"Several men of the town saw you meeting with Mary Witherslack,"

"Mistress Burnley?"

"You know what I'm talking about, Godwin. I don't want to make myself plainer."

"What you imply and what happened are two different things."

"Have you lain with her?"

"No!"

"Do you expect me to believe that? You were seen in the wood lying together!"

"It is a lie! A damnable lie!"

Talbot's face grew redder until it was quite apparent that he would explode from the rage within him. "You protest too much, Godwin. You tremble. Is your vocation and your soul worth the Jezebel, this Whore of Babylon? Because of your assignation, Erland Frankewell bled to death. Your betrayal of his friendship and his understanding with Mary Burnley brought on this most unfortunate and unhappy event!"

Godwin felt the air rush out of his lungs, and he gasped, feeling faint and sick to his stomach. "I do assure you, sir," he said when he had recovered; "I may love her, but when has taking a walk in plain sight of the village become a carnal sin? You wrong an innocent lady! I have no doubt you are the author of these vicious lies! For that is what they are: vicious and cruel lies meant to disgrace and damn someone who has done nothing to anyone in this village!"

Godwin's impassioned denouncement came as no surprise to Talbot, who was inwardly glad that the stupid fool was falling in love with Mary Burnley. It was a means to rid himself of the educated, liberal pest.

The news of Erland's suicide reached Mary at the same time Godwin learned of it. Emily took it upon herself to tell her daughter and was disappointed that the girl showed no grief. Perhaps, she thought, looking around the neat little cottage, the stories of Mary becoming Godwin's lover were fact. For when Mary came from the barn, the shining brightness of her eyes and her radiance, her happy smile, all faded when she saw her mother and made Emily think that Mary was expecting Godwin. Cora returned home at the same time with the news, but she wisely kept her tongue and hurried into the cottage to set a tea at Mary's quiet request. To Emily's morbid delight, Godwin appeared almost as soon as she was settled with a cup of tea and biscuits.

"Mister Herrold, I suppose you have come to share the unfortunate news making its way around Knowstone?" Emily stated flatly and without preamble or greeting when Mary brought him into the room. "Erland Frankewell is dead!"

"He's dead?" Mary gasped. She sat hard on the settee and waved away Emily, who moved to comfort her.

"That's not all," Emily sniffed. She then took great delight in recounting the numerous stories she'd heard (and embellished) of Mary's illicit love with the curate of St. Ælfgiva's Church, how they met in St. Edmund Wood, and lay together like pagans and how they conspired together to break Erland's heart.

"Mistress Witherslack, do you take comfort in slandering your daughter with these lies?" Godwin interrupted her.

"And what do you say to these charges? To these lies?" Mary demanded of Godwin quietly. She had not shed a single tear, and he noted that with some satisfaction.

"I refute them, of course."

"And will you deny them openly?"

"In church on Sunday if you'd like."

"That is the shortest way to suspicion, Godwin. To some, protestations mean guilt. I would rather you say nothing."

"Then I shall say nothing if that is what you wish."

"You must do it for yourself."

Emily cleared her throat now to remind them they were not alone. She watched their faces and how their eyes blazed and how Mary's breast rose and fell quicker every moment she looked at him. She couldn't take her eyes away. They were both lying; she knew it!

Godwin wanted so much to take Mary in his arms and tell her she was not to blame, and nor was he, that the truth would prove their innocence, but he prudently kept his distance. "I will go now. If you have any need…"

"I shall be fine, Mister Herrold." She didn't look at him.

"Good evening, then."

Once he was gone, Emily sighed, and in that sigh were a thousand words. "I wish I could believe you, but, after all that happened in the past, well,"

"I am nothing of what you make me!" Mary snapped. "You shame us both!"

"The fool is in love with you. Don't you see it?"

"I see what I want to see."

"And so does all of Knowstone, my dear. Perhaps now you will leave for good. It would be best. You can go to Chester to live with my sister—or wherever we might find a remote corner of England that has yet to hear of you!"

The door slammed behind Emily, and Cora crept over to throw the bar and bolt it. When she turned to clear away the tea, Mary took her hands, looking at her with sad, frightened eyes.

"I'll leave tomorrow evening when the London coach arrives," Mary whispered, holding back her tears.

"It's what everyone wants, Miss!"

"Of course it is. It is one battle I have lost."

"Where will we go?"

"I shall go alone, Cora. Please don't cry! I will give you an allowance to keep you for many months. I still have money put aside," Mary consoled the weeping girl with an embrace. "I will go as suddenly as I returned, and there won't be a soul in Knowstone who won't know it and secretly rejoice!"

Cora sniffed back her tears and wiped her eyes on her sleeve. "There is one who will mourn, Miss, someone other than me."

"Yes," Mary whispered as she reached for the pebble in her apron. "I know."

CHAPTER 14

SHE WOULD GO as suddenly as she returned and knew there'd be a few souls in Knowstone who would rejoice. But, as Cora hinted, there was one who would not.

The London coach would be at the inn by six o'clock in the evening, and Mary spent the day of her departure going about business as if nothing had happened and as if it were an ordinary day. Chores and meals were shared with Cora. She worked at her loom and embroidered Jane Frankewell's wedding linens, went over the account books, and finally, packed for her journey. She decided to take only a small satchel of her belongings. The rest she would send for when settled, for Mary decided that she'd go to Cambridge, find her own lodgings and make her own way, begin anew. When Cora and Mrs. Teamer asked why, she said, "Because I've never been there."

Once farewells were exchanged among her neighbors in Bottle Street, Mary went to the church. She slipped into the sanctuary and walked through the haze of candle smoke that hung in the air, the scent of incense and tallow, to the choir where she knelt, and for the first time in many months, actually prayed.

"Holy Father, you know what is in my heart, you know my desperation, you know before I even ask what it is that I desire most."

She remained on her knees, keeping her eyes fixed on the dull windows, whose usually brilliant colors were muddy from the fading light, and finally to the wooden Christ nailed against the screen before the altar. She waited, hoping for a sign, a word of encouragement, but all she heard was the distant sound of the coachman's horn. Sighing resolutely, she took the bit of glass from her pocket and placed it on the altar, and left Knowstone. It caught the morning sun hours later when Godwin entered the sanctuary to set up for morning prayer. He noticed it at once and frowned, glanced about, and it was after the service that he dared to ask one of the women about Mary.

"Oh, that one!" said Mistress Galthwaite. "I've not seen her for weeks, not since she left Hazelwick and went to take up in Street End Cottage in Bottle Street. I don't mind saying that she's a strange one, what with all the business about her father and now Master Erland."

"Thank you," Godwin replied impatiently. It wasn't anything he hadn't already heard from most of the women in Knowstone. How deep the jealousy and resentment ran! He had hopes for better news when he saw Cora.

"Cora! Good morning," he greeted the maid.

"Sir," she replied with a curtsey.

"Cora, how is your mistress?"

"She's gone, sir. She went to Cambridge last night. Took the coach."

"For what purpose? No, I'm a fool to ask because I know. But Cambridge and not Oxford?" Godwin mused aloud, a frown creasing his brow. When he noticed Cora's look of concern and worry, he smiled and said, "Thank you, Cora. May I come by this afternoon? I was looking in on Mister Dowling and Mistress Teamer and thought perhaps…"

"There's naught else I can tell you, sir. But if you need to come for a cup of tea, you're welcome."

Godwin nodded and glanced down the high street, expecting, perhaps hoping, to see Mary Burnley coming up from Hazelwick, a smile ready on her red lips, the light of life in her eyes, those tokens for Godwin only and no other.

∞

THE ROUTINE WAS the same; it was as if nothing had happened in the intervening weeks. Godwin set off for Bottle Street one

Sunday afternoon and was greeted by villagers without indifference or suspicion. Here he was accepted and not judged. As usual, the last stop was at Street End Cottage. He tried to hide his disappointment when Cora answered his knock and smiled shyly at Godwin; he hoped Mary would have returned from Cambridge and that her sudden flight was nothing more than a holiday to see a friend.

"Have you taken supper, Mister Herrold?" Cora asked when she invited him in.

"Mistress Teamer made sure I won't starve until morning," Godwin jested weakly. He looked around, and his heart leaped when he saw a familiar shawl, a vase full of bluebells. Surely...

"You'll take tea, then? I've set the kettle to boil. We can use the new china cups the mistress bought," Cora said as she went to a shelf above the hearth.

"New tea set? Is she home then?"

"No sir,"

"Oh."

"She sent them from Cambridge when the removers came for her loom and things."

"Are you well?"

"Mistress Burnley pays the rent for the cottage and has promised to visit. I'm to join her when she finds a house of her own."

Biscuits, tea cakes, and a fragrant black tea were set before Godwin at the table, and Cora stood by expectantly.

"Won't you join me, Cora?" Godwin asked after he'd taken a biscuit and a sip of tea and glanced up to see her smiling nervously. "I know Mistress Burnley holds to no ceremony." Cora sat down and poured a cup of tea, and helped herself to one of the cakes. "I suppose you know why she left?"

"It's no surprise to anyone."

"Was she in love with him? Still?"

"Oh no, sir! It was plain to me that she loved another— if you know what I mean."

Godwin tried to hide his smile behind his teacup. "Yes, there was talk. Erland's death upset many plans."

"It's better he's gone, Sir!"

"Cora!"

"He said he murdered you, and then he hinted at killing Mister Burnley, too! She said as much to me the day after it happened! He said those evil things to hurt Mistress Burnley! Knowing him, he took pleasure in it, too. And if what he said about her late husband if that was true, and if he did poison Mister Burnley, well, I think he deserves what punishment God gives!" the girl said.

A scolding for lack of Christian charity was on his lips, but Godwin kept his silence. *So Justin Burnley was a victim of Erland's jealousy, too?* "Have you any word from her, Cora?"

"A message came just two days ago," Cora said. "A peddler from Crewe came round and brought a message. She says she's taken a position as a seamstress in a tailor's shop. When she has enough money, she's going to rent a shop and send for me. She said she's found peace."

"She is happy I take it," Godwin pronounced sadly.

"She could be happy, Sir," Cora said as she poured another cup of tea and smiled at him. "Cambridge is far, isn't it, but not a world away?"

Five to seven days' ride, if that, and if the weather holds, Godwin thought. He accepted the tea cake Cora offered and started to make plans that were still foremost in his thoughts as he officiated at Evensong and when he quietly left the vicarage at midnight. Mrs. Talbot heard the clatter of hoofbeats on the cobblestones and got out of bed to look, parting the lace curtains just in time to see Godwin disappear into the eastern night.

"Stupid boy!" she hissed.

"Hunh? Wha's tha?" Talbot murmured from his pillow.

"Just a moment now," his wife said as she lit a candle and went out, coming back as she said, in a moment, slamming the bedroom door. Talbot sat up and yawned.

"What's got you so damned upset that you interrupt what little sleep I get, eh, Marjorie?"

"He's gone! That stupid, reckless, wastrel!"

"A name for this fool, perhaps?"

"Who do you think? Godwin! I saw him leave. All of his belongings are gone save the new collars. And there's a letter for you."

Mrs. Talbot threw the letter at her husband and climbed back into bed. "You know what this means?"

Talbot smiled when he read the brief letter of resignation. "It means I may do as I like. Go back to sleep. I know I shall sleep soundly for once!"

"Are you as big a fool as Godwin Herrold, Charles? He will go to the Bishop! He will pour his heart out to the Bishop and everything, everything—"

"He knows nothing, Marjorie. Go to sleep. Tomorrow will be a splendid day because God wills it!"

Before Marjorie Talbot rolled onto her side to face the window, she pummeled Talbot's shoulder, and for good measure thumped him with a pillow. Sleep did not come as easily for her as it did for her husband. She was still awake and wondering about this latest turn of events when the sun rose and the sounds of morning with it. Marjorie avoided the obsequious greetings and artificial concern for her wellbeing when she entered the church by the side door as was her right, casting frowns and glances about when she sat in her usual place below the pulpit. When the organist started to play the opening hymn and Godwin hadn't taken his place at the prayer desk, heads turned, frowns creased brows, and whispers made it evident that something was wrong.

"Is Mister Herrold ill?" John Merrow inquired kindly of Mrs. Talbot as they greeted one another after the service. Talbot was ready to crow over what he considered a victory over Satan when Marjorie said, "He's gone to Canterbury to see his parents. His mother is quite ill."

"How sad, how unfortunate! But how fortunate she is to

have such a loving and doting son!" Katherine Merrow exclaimed. "You must give him our regards when he returns."

"If he returns," Talbot added. And turning to his wife, hissed, "You do know his mother is dead these last five years?"

Marjorie frowned and, under her breath wished Godwin Herrold in hell.

Emily Witherslack smiled when she heard the news. Talbot was stirring his tea in that irritating manner while telling a somewhat different story than was going around Knowstone. She stared at the motes of dust in the bar of afternoon sunlight that sliced over the Turkish carpet Mary had purchased in Oxford. Silly, ugly thing! She'd give it to the rag and bone man on Wednesday next. Better to have a bare wood floor and go cold in the winter than to be reminded of disappointment.

". . . and so Mistress Talbot thrusts this hastily-penned letter at me while I'm still trying to wake. It was a letter of resignation. He didn't say why or where he was going."

"You do know where he's gone, Talbot. And why. He's gone looking for her!" Emily said.

Talbot coughed. "Your daughter."

"Much luck may he have! No one knows where she's gone. No matter how I coax and bribe that silly girl Cora, she won't tell."

"Perhaps she doesn't know?"

"She knows! How else could she keep Street End Cottage? She knows. More to the point, Godwin Herrold knows."

Godwin Herrold didn't know.

He didn't know where Mary Burnley was other than she'd gone to Cambridge and knew a peddler from Crewe well enough to have sent messages to and from Knowstone with regularity over the month since her departure. After a delay of three days due to a sudden squall, he arrived in the city and took a room at the Eagle and Child. While soaking in a bath, Godwin planned a strategy. If, after five days, he'd not discovered Mary, he would continue on to Canterbury and present himself to the Archbishop. Surely the letter he'd sent would have reached him by now. Then there would be a more difficult interview with his father. For that, he would need better arguments and excuses to explain his failures.

How many disappointments could a man withstand in a lifetime, Godwin wondered; how many could one man bestow?

He felt he'd failed Mary Burnley, or at the very least, scared her off by proclaiming his love for her too soon. But she did love him. Godwin smiled as he remembered her kisses and the taste of her mouth and skin, the feel of her against him. So many missteps, so many mistakes. Mary would not be one of them.

An hour before sunset, Godwin was strolling about Cambridge when he heard the bells of a local church and glanced up at the sky. Evensong. He followed the sound and arrived at Saint Bene't's Church, just across the lane from his inn. Once his sight was adjusted to the dusky light, he noticed the fine embroidered frontal and pulpit hangings, the burse, and veil draping a chalice and paten on the altar. But of course, this was a place of renown, a church known for centuries for its Opus Anglicum, the English embroidery made famous by nuns of the convent before the Conquest.

There was a scattering of people in the nave, perhaps six or seven. Godwin's attention went to three ladies who sat in the quire, their hands folded over squares of folded cloth. No doubt the altar guild.

How glorious were the prayers and canticles when they weren't part of an hour's labor; when one didn't have to worry about the criticism once the candles were snuffed and the last reedy notes of hymns floated up into the eleventh-century timber and stone and dissolved with the smoke of candles and incense. Godwin was content to sit and watch the priest and musician clear away the sanctuary just as he had done so many times at St. Ælfgiva's Church. Hurry up and get away to supper to find some privacy and quiet. Was that how it was for them, too?

Godwin finally rose and walked to the altar steps to offer his reverence when he noticed one of the ladies smiling.

"Welcome. You are a stranger here?" she greeted.

"A traveler, passing through," Godwin lied.

"Not many come to this little place. It is forgotten."

"But surely a treasure," he said, stepping closer, and it was then he noticed the familiar embroidery pattern on the altar fair cloth, the repeating motif of rose and cross, rose and cross.

"Some of the most beautiful work we've seen in years," the lady said when she noticed Godwin's preoccupation.

"Do you know the artisan?"

"I do not. It comes from a shop nearby, or so I'm told."

Godwin studied the pattern and again, then smiled and said good evening. Another part of the mystery was solved. In the morning, he discovered there were many shops in Cambridge that sold needlework and embroidery. The first day was a disappointment and found him back at St. Bene't's in the evening. The friendly woman of last evening was again seated with her companions in the quire, and she nodded when he slipped into a pew for the service.

"Excuse me, Mistress?" Godwin said by way of greeting later.

"So you've returned," she answered. "You delight in our treasure."

"I wonder if you would tell me the name of the shop where this linen was purchased?"

"You are preoccupied," she said but not unkindly. "I am Veronica Lathrop."

"I am—" Godwin paused and then decided it was best to tell the truth. "Godwin Herrold, former curate at St. Ælfgiva's Church in Cheshire."

Her eyes lit. "Ah! You've come to study at the university?"

"I look for a friend."

"The talented seamstress, I think?"

"The same." Godwin felt the heat of a blush rise up in his face and returned her smile. "There are so many shops in

Cambridge, and my search today came to naught."

Veronica turned to her companions in the quire stalls. "Anne, Charlotte, do you know the shop where Father Randolph purchases the fair linen?"

"Mister Siward's shop in Hollywell Street."

Veronica turned back to Godwin and said, "There! I wish you good fortune, Godwin Herrold."

CHAPTER 15

MISTER SIWARD'S ESTABLISHMENT in Hollywell Street was not where Godwin expected to find Mary Burnley: it was a dark and shabby little shop among many in a squalid and dark street attracting the poorest and working poor of Cambridge. Cheaply-made imitations of better quality goods shown in the expensive shops along the high street decorated window stalls that needed washing and cobwebs cleared so the dresses and shirts could be seen in the dim light offered between buildings leaning against one another to make an arch. Cheerfully painted window frames and doors would have looked out of place here; the peeling paint and warped wood were what one would expect.

The proprietor of Siward's was a colorless man in garish and brightly-colored clothes. If an orange brocaded topcoat and violet waistcoat of corduroy were to be believed, this man wore them proudly with dove-gray breeches and buckled shoes the same color. When the doorbell chimed, and Godwin entered, glancing around expectantly, he snapped a lorgnette to his jaundiced eyes and nodded in greeting.

"Welcome to Siward's," the gentleman said. "We have the most affordable and fashionable clothing for students of the university. I am Telford Siward at your service."

"Good day, sir. I am looking for a seamstress you may have in your employ," Godwin said. "Mistress Mary Burnley."

"Mary Burnley! Ah, well, she's not here at the moment. I sent her to Madame Jonquil's shop in the high street for a length of lace. Perhaps you will take a moment to inspect our cravats and gloves? You'll find nothing comparable in London."

Godwin looked at the dusty gloves in the filthy display case and said, "I can believe you, sir, but my business is with Mistress Burnley. Good day."

Godwin dusted down his sleeves and shoulders once out in the street as if removing contamination and looked up and down the lane. If this Madame Jonquil kept a shop in the high street, it wouldn't be too difficult to find, and it wasn't—except that it was shuttered and looked as if it had been vacant for weeks. Frustrated, Godwin went back to Siward's.

"You've reconsidered our doeskin gloves, then?" Siward greeted.

"Another time, sir. You neglected to tell me that Madame Jonquil's shop is vacant and looks as if it has been so for some time."

"Did I say Madame Jonquil? Ah! Mistress Burnley went to Cherry Hinton to Madame Jonquil, who makes lace."

"When will she return?"

"Tomorrow—I think."

"Tomorrow, then. Good day. Again."

This interview was conducted several times more when Godwin, ready to admit defeat and continue on to Canterbury, decided to visit Siward's one last time. As usual, the doorbell announced him sweetly; the same dusty garments stood on wicker reed forms, and the display case had a new layer of dust. Where would she be today, Godwin wondered; at Pevensey or Norwich? Ely? Winchester? Had she been sent to sew buttons on a waistcoat? Deck a bonnet with ribbons? He was ready for a quarrel with Siward when he thought something was off.

The difference was the young woman behind the counter.

One of the shutters had actually been pushed open so that sunlight managed to find a way into the shop and did little to improve its appearance, but the sun on the woman was another matter. Mary Burnley was cast in shadows like one of Leonardo's Madonnas, the play of *chiaroscuro* softening her already beautiful features. Godwin fell in love with her again, just gazing at her. He committed everything to memory and noted the new—a new hairstyle, a new dress, a new weariness. The needle in her hand moved slowly, mechanically, as if she was a loom and someone was pushing heddles and dampening the reeds. Needlework was her faith, she jested once when they walked through the castle ruins, but her lugubrious movements and sighs were telling.

Godwin found his voice and said, "Mistress, forgive me, but I am a persistent suitor." Expecting a rebuff, he was nearly toppled by the speed of flight when she ran into his arms. "I take it my efforts to find you were not in vain!" he laughed after they kissed.

෨

THEY STROLLED ARM in arm through the ancient city and shared their news after weeks of separation, little vignettes of life in Bottle Street and at the church, how Mary found both employment and boarding, and how she was settling into life in Cambridge. Would she attend lectures at the university if permitted? She didn't know, but she was intrigued. Both were overwhelmed by happiness, and each expressed delight in Godwin's perseverance. It was like a faery tale come to life, Mary suggested, but he would know and know well that she had no need of rescue. A companion to share her days? Perhaps.

Later in the day, they went to the Eagle and Child for supper. Mary noticed Godwin's preoccupation with and vigil on the church across the street as they sat by a window and waited for their meal. "The Lord is a gentle lover, patient, and understanding," she murmured, covering his hand with hers.

"What, my heart? Hmm?" Godwin answered, startled out of his reverie.

"I fear I have compromised your vocation. You will be disgraced and have to answer for your un-priestly actions. And yet I know that Mother Church will always be your mistress and love, and I am content with that," Mary's voice was low so that no one else could hear. When she reached up to touch his face, he kissed the hand and took it in his own.

"You are not the cause. You are the marvelous effect of what grace can do," he whispered.

"But what have you done?" Mary ventured. "It could not have been easy for you to leave Knowstone."

Godwin bristled and reached for the tankard of ale before him. "I should have left months ago," he muttered, and then to Mary said, "I went looking for you. To be certain you were safe and well."

"Dear God, does Talbot know you're gone? I am afraid for you!" Mary whispered and held his hand more firmly.

"I left a letter of resignation,"

"Godwin!"

"It was only a matter of time before I left on my own accord, or Talbot found a way to throw me out—although he has no recourse for his complaints against my work and my person, real or imagined."

"Are you certain?"

"I'm on my way to Canterbury."

"To see the archbishop?" she gasped.

He nodded. "The bishop of Chester would not give me a fair hearing. I know the archbishop, and despite my faults, he will give me an audience. I will speak to him about Knowstone, about what I've learned while curate at St. Ælfgiva's. I will have justice for the people in Bottle Street, for those Talbot and his accomplices injured. Then I will discern my future."

"I'm glad for you!"

"Come with me," Godwin said but moved away as the serving girl brought plates of roast lamb and potatoes, carrots, and mugs of ale. When she left, he reached for Mary's hand again. "Come with me. I'll have more strength for this if you are beside me."

"This is dangerous!" Mary whispered.

"The danger is not to us. We are together, and that is all that matters."

Mary smiled sadly. "How will it look to have the woman

most people call your harlot and your lover following you about from appointment to appointment?"

"Is that what I am? Your lover?" he asked with delight.

"It is what everyone in Knowstone thinks," Mary sighed, and then after a pause, added, "It is the truth. It is what I would hope."

"I would rather you be my wife, and for that, I have hoped—"

A trio of university students made a noisy entrance and took the only table left in the common room, inconveniently close to Godwin and Mary. While they laughed and disputed philosophy and science, the couple from Knowstone dined quietly, and when they rose to leave, one of the students nodded in greeting and said, "Sir, your wife is too fair for you. I think she is too beautiful for the world! What a warm bed you must enjoy, hey?" This was followed by approving raps on the table and tankards raised. Rather than correct him, Godwin offered his courtesy, and when he and Mary were alone in the vestibule near the stairs, he pulled her closed and kissed her.

"Shall we prove him right, Mary?" Godwin whispered huskily between kisses that were growing passionate. "Will you marry me? Be my wife in every sense of the word? There's the church across the way!"

"Yes," she answered breathlessly. "But now I must go. Come tomorrow to Hollywell Street. If it is at all possible, I will marry you tomorrow."

"Tomorrow is not soon enough, for I would have you in my bed tonight and every night after that!"

"Shall I stay with you, then?" she asked after a moment of studying his face.

"As much as I would want that, Mary, it can't be. Why give credence to gossips? We must stay above the speculation and rumor."

"Tomorrow?" she whispered after a last kiss.

Godwin released her and watched Mary spirit away in the

twilight settling over Cambridge, her pale pink frock like a candle flame as it caught the last of the light as Mary hurried home, wherever that was. Surely not the odious Mr. Siward's! As soon as she was out of sight, Godwin went across the street to St. Bene't's Church and asked to see the rector.

ഗ

MARY WAS BREATHLESS and giddy when she arrived at her lodgings with Mrs. Jane in Bride's Street. *Bride's Street!* It was amusing, she thought, as she entered the sitting room and found her landlady reading. Mrs. Jane glanced up and removed her spectacles, saying, "I trow! This is the first time I've seen a smile on your face, Mistress Burnley. Whatever has changed your opinion of the world?"

"Life!" Mary giggled. "How glorious life is, Mistress Jane!" She was still wrapped in this incredible happiness an hour later when she was in her bath, and there was a knock on the door. Mrs. Jane entered with a letter and a single rose, the palest pink of blooms that was perfection. The message was brief:

Saturday at eleven o'clock. Saint Bene't's Church. I love you!

Mary slid further into the bath and hugged herself. Two days to wait, but it was enough. It would be the longest forty-eight hours in her life.

Ah, life!

ഗ

WHAT A STRANGE wedding supper this is, Godwin thought as he looked around the table in Mrs. Jane's dining room. Mr. Siward, Mrs. Jane, Veronica Lathrop, and The Reverend Mister Poperly, people he had known for barely a week celebrating his marriage to 'their Mary,' and he was quite comfortable with it.

"Will you stay awhile in Cambridge, Mister Herrold?" asked Poperly, filling Godwin's glass with wine. "We are fond of your wife and hope that she will continue her trade with us. I've never seen finer linen and embroidery work, nor a finer young woman. To Mistress Herrold!"

"Mistress Herrold!" the party exclaimed.

"To my wife," Godwin said softly, raising his glass to Mary. "As to whether Mistress Herrold and I shall we stay here, Mister Poperly, I must first go to Canterbury on business, but I see no reason to make Mary leave since she seems content here with such amiable friends."

"I will go with you, Godwin," Mary said. "I may ply my needle wherever I am, but, if the choice were mine, I'd like a shop in the high street if my husband has no objection to my earning a living while he does the same."

Laughter circulated around the table and Godwin offered another toast.

"When the children start to come, you'll have enough on your hands," Mrs. Jane commented.

"But surely it would be a possibility? We live in a time when our possibilities seem endless," Mary replied. "And where else but in Cambridge, a great university city?"

Mary, however, sounded not as hopeful hours later when she went with Godwin to The Eagle and Child.

"It was kind of your friends to host our bridal supper," Godin commented as he led the way upstairs.

"You have no objection to my earning a living?" she asked. "I fear I may have sounded too industrious and independent from the knowing smiles and telling looks I received. I'm sorry to have embarrassed and scandalized you!"

"Let them think it was the effect of the wine," he answered as he pushed open the door and lifted her easily into his arms to carry her across the threshold. "I will have my wife happy and content. Besides," Godwin added as he let her slide against him to her feet, "we don't know what the outcome of my meeting in Canterbury will be, and at least we'll have some income if it doesn't embarrass you to have a redundant husband if I'm unsuccessful. Do you have an objection to that, my love?"

"No, because I know the archbishop will listen to you," Mary replied.

How very happy we are, Godwin thought hours later when

the moon set and the sky was turning with the dawn. How perfectly we match.

Godwin drew his sleeping wife close and put to memory every contour and aspect of her perfect body, wept tears of joy for the dewy softness of her naked skin against him now that they were truly one, and wondered at his good fortune to have this woman.

There was nothing like this on Earth. To lie in a woman's arms and feel her body against his, to discover mysteries and pleasures, to hold her closer and closer until that sweet, divine moment came and rather than rest, want it all the more, to ride a tide of delicious sleep and then wake and have the desire again, to know that it was shared and love reciprocated.

He prayed that this profound and passionate love would never leave them.

಄

WE ARE HAPPY. I am happy, Mary thought.

Sitting before a mirror at the dressing table, Mary brushed out her hair, comfortable already in her station and circumstance. It seemed quite natural to sit in this charming room with the flowered and striped wallpaper and white linens, the lace curtains. It was natural with Godwin sitting on the bed removing his boots and jacket and then stretching out for a moment of peace after a day of planning. The sun was burning hotly into the room and cast a warm, orange glow. The tinny ring of a clock somewhere told her it was five in the afternoon, and she had been married for more than a day. Mary held up her left hand and admired the gold band on her third finger, how the sunlight captured the ancient engraving of love knots that encircled it.

"In memory of the lady Ælfgyva," Godwin murmured when he purchased it from the jeweler's shop in Watling Street. "She would have worn such a beautiful thing had she married for love."

Godwin was dozing when the maid came up to offer a hot bath and fresh linens for the good reverend's wife. He listened as the water was poured, and the women spoke in whispers. The gentle rise and fall of the water, the sweet sound of her voice as she sang softly, and the scent of perfumed steam rising in their bedroom.

"And so we are man and wife, Mistress Herrold," Godwin said drowsily, eyes closed.

"So we are, Mister Herrold. A joyful thing it is, too. Has it been just a day, sir?"

"A memorable day, an even more splendid night. Another splendid night to anticipate. Let that sustain us when we leave for Canterbury tomorrow."

"You never said why you left Canterbury."

"No, I didn't."

"Why did you?"

Godwin took in the scent of soap and listened as a sponge or brush rode up and down skin he knew would be soft, warm, and glistening. Perhaps he should share the bath and save worries for another time. He could explain tomorrow when they were in the coach.

"Godwin?"

No, better to tell all.

"A difference of opinion where it concerned a lady I loved and marriage."

The room was suddenly silent, and then Mary resumed washing.

"Not much different from the present situation, I think?"

"A world of difference, Mary. You married for love the first time—and this last, I pray. I married to acquire property and a good station in society to please my father. My bride hated me. Then I became a sport for her, her curiosity. She was charming, beautiful—I won't deny she was, but not as beautiful as you, Mary—and from a family of influence that enriched my father's fortunes with her substantial dowry. And she was evil."

"Was? Then you're—"

"No different from you. Until yesterday, I was a

widower."

The silence that followed was unbearable.

What a fool I am to bring up this painful subject! Godwin thought. He wanted to share it eventually, but on their honeymoon? When they should be in each other's arms in this bed?

God damn me for this curse of honesty!

Mary was so quiet now; was she weeping or simmering with anger that her husband decided to spoil what he hoped would be another exquisite night of lovemaking by opening a wound he'd hoped was closed and healed?

Godwin opened his eyes. He was afraid to get off the bed and walk around the screen to look at her for what he might see.

"Go on. We're not meant to have secrets," Mary finally said.

"Her death was, well, it wasn't as romantic as consumption or childbed fever. She was strangled by her lover when she tried to leave him. You see, I was a cuckold. I wasn't sent down from Canterbury. I walked away. I simply opened the rectory door and rode away. They found me at a tavern near King's Lynn. I wanted passage to France or die of drink. The Archbishop thought it was nonsense and sent me to think things over in Knowstone and do penance."

Godwin paused, the sponge brushing back and forth, the water rising and falling. But she was silent.

He continued: "At first, it was the worst kind of purgatory, hell even, but then I met you. You were like nothing and no one in the village, and from the way the people of Knowstone treated you, I thought you were a fairy creature or sylph. And then we met, and we spoke, and I was beguiled from that moment. When you told me about your ancestress and the knight, and when I saw you with the neighbors in Bottle Street, the children in the market square, I believed you were an angel without wings, or if you had them, they were invisible to me."

"You flatter me, sir!"

"I heard stories and saw the way the men in Knowstone looked at you. Talbot expounded on a sinful nature he was sure you had, though I could not see it—and if it was there, I did not want to see it. That Erland should kill himself for love of you. I refused to believe that. I began to think that perhaps you were like my late wife after all and that I would be a fool again if we loved one another. Now it makes sense. I understand perfectly. I would be a fool not to love you or want you, Mary!"

He didn't hear Mary come from the bath or kneel beside the bed. Godwin opened his eyes when he felt Mary's fingers tracing his tears. She leaned over to kiss him, and he responded gently, pulling her scented, warm body towards his. She was still damp, and the bed robe flannel clung to her skin so that her wonderful curves were apparent and enticing.

"My darling Godwin! Think no more of it."

Godwin reached up and kissed the dewy skin of her exposed neck and shoulders down to her breasts. "When my father discovers what I've done, I'll have nothing to give you, Mary," he murmured between kisses and love bites; "I'll have no fortune, no inheritance. I'll be disowned because to his eyes and way of thinking, I will have failed. You see, I chose a path none other in my family had taken. I became a priest, and I found that God still didn't care. Men of the cloth are just men. We have no special grace."

"You do have grace! Ah, the good that you do, my love!" Mary whispered. "You gave me this ring. You give yourself. Now we have each other."

Mary moved away to draw the curtains across the window. The room was dusky, but there was enough light for Godwin to see her silhouette against the window, watch as she came to the bed again, and slipped the flannel robe from her shoulders before tumbling into his welcome arms.

CHAPTER 16

"WE SHALL HAVE to leave this bed . . . eventually."

"But darling Mary, if we stay here, we avoid disappointment in Canterbury."

"Then let us find a bed in Canterbury. What do you say?"

"I say that I love you."

Mary turned in Godwin's arms to receive his kiss. They lay entwined after their coupling, heartbeats slowing and breathing coming deep and long as their bodies relaxed. Here was another morning they greeted without having slept the night before. In the purple shadows, Godwin saw her bright eyes and the curve of her naked shoulders draped by the blankets and coverlets. He let a hand slip under the down coverlet and ride over the silken skin. She was a mystery and marvel to him, and he trembled at the touch of her.

"I suppose if we don't leave now, they'll find two old and withered people buried under these quilts in thirty years' time," Mary sighed. She got up and took the sheets and covers with her so that Godwin resembled Botticelli's naked sleeping Mars. Mary paused to admire her god and lover before dressing. Godwin was roused from his sleep by a gentle blow to the head with a pillow. "As much as I would delight to admire your beauty all day and take pleasure from it, Godwin my heart, you cannot go to Canterbury clothed only in God's grace," she teased. Godwin stretched wearily and finally climbed out of bed. An hour later, they boarded an Eastern coach to Canterbury. The euphoria and ease of the last two days ebbed the closer they came to their destination. Godwin noticed how tense Mary was when he put an arm around her.

"How are you, my dear?" he murmured, kissing her hair.

"What will we do if the archbishop will not give you a fair hearing?"

"I haven't thought of that yet. I hope that my letter will have reached him by now and that it will open his eyes to clerical abuses."

She was rigid now and abruptly shifted as if being so close pained her. "It cannot be otherwise, I am sure of it," Mary said, a brittle smile on her lips. Then she declared with enthusiasm, "How fortunate not just for me that you came to Knowstone but to the poor and lonely in Bottle Street! Whatever Mister Talbot's complaints about you, they were unwarranted, for I have seen and am a beneficiary of your goodness."

She started fidgeting with her lace gloves so that there was an eyelet where none had been before. When Mary realized what she'd done, she clasped her hands together and sighed. Perhaps it is fatigue, Godwin thought as he moved away. We've had precious little sleep of late. When we arrive, I'll go immediately to the archbishop, and that will give her time alone and time to rest.

Godwin was true to his word. They took rooms at the Cathedral Gate Hotel, and as soon as he knew Mary was sleeping, he washed up and then departed quietly for his appointment. The thud of the door closing woke Mary, and she sleepily gazed at her surroundings.

"Godwin?" she called, peering out into the still dark bedroom. "Darling?"

The only response was the sound of a milk wagon trundling up the street.

Mary burrowed deep into the bed and sighed contentedly. He'd be back soon, she was sure with good news, and they would breakfast and talk about the future, make plans. She would ask the concierge for a lemon cake, which was Godwin's favorite. As she drifted back to the first restful sleep she'd enjoyed in months, Mary found herself dreaming of another time in her life that had moments of sweetness like those in the past week and when the future looked just as bright.

"You called for me, sir?"

Mary had rapped on the door of her father's study and waited as The Rev. Percy Witherslack finished writing, most certainly tomorrow's sermon. He looked up, startling eyes the color of aquamarines flickering as they darted up and down, taking measure of his daughter.

"Come in," Witherslack said, though it was more of a bark than an invitation.

Even obedient, Mary entered and closed the door behind her. She made a curtsey before coming to stand at her father's desk. Witherslack's eyes darted up and down again, then cleared his throat. Mary clasped her hands before her.

"I've just been to Saltfield—"

"Did I give you leave to speak?"

"No, Father,"

"Did I give you leave to speak?"

Each syllable was clipped as if struck from ice.

Mary clasped her hands together as tightly as she could and looked down at her boots. They were her best pair and covered with dirt and mud from traipsing through St. Edmund Wood. She moved just a bit so that the hems of her skirt and petticoats would hide them from sight.

Witherslack stabbed his quill into its stand and closed the folio before him. He spent some time organizing the books and papers on the desk, and all the while Mary kept her head down.

"What business had you at Saltfield?" he demanded.

Mary's head shot up and then back down when she saw her father's stern expression and the cold eyes. "Lady Isobel made an invitation, sir."

"Is that new? Where did you get that?"

Witherslack pointed at the lace shawl draped about Mary's lovely swan-like neck and covering her low-cut bodice.

One of Mary's hands involuntarily rested on the soft fabric as she said, "It is a gift to me from Lady Isobel."

"Why would she give you something? You are nothing to her."

"Today is my birthday, sir."

"What? Speak up!"

"It is my birthday, Father."

"Fifteen years," sniffed Witherslack as if there was a foul odor in the room. "And you are not yet married."

"No, sir."

Father and daughter stared at one another, and then Mary resumed her meditation on her partially-hidden boots.

"You will return the shawl. It is too fine for you. It screams of pride and vanity."

"But sir! It is a gift. Surely you will let me keep it? Lady Isobel is dear to me and I to her, and so she said."

"And why?" Witherslack hissed.

Mary hesitated and then smiled, saying, "Erland Frankewell wishes to pay court. We have been friends for most of our lives. He desires to marry me."

"What do you desire?"

"To marry Erland Frankewell," Mary said and then added hastily, "because I love him, and he loves me. We have pledged our hearts."

Witherslack cleared his throat and flipped through the pages of a Bible, turning to a page. He tapped it. "Read it."

It was in Greek. Mary creased her brow and studied the words and then finally, "'I will . . . not . . . punish your daughters . . . when they commit . . . whoredom, nor your spouses when they . . . commit adultery: for, for themselves are . . . separated . . . with whores, and they sacrifice with harlots?'"

"Just so." Witherslack hissed and pulled the Bible away from her.

"These are the words of Hosea. What have they to do with an engagement to Erland Frankewell?"

"Your education is wanting. We will take a walk after supper. Go."

Mary curtseyed and left the study. Walks with her father

meant stimulating conversation and tutelage, which always fascinated her and gave her time away from her disapproving mother, whose pastimes were silly: holding teas for the wealthy wives of Knowstone and gossiping about members of the Royal Family, putting of airs and flirting. She and her father would walk to the castle or abbey ruins, and Mary would receive a lesson in history or theology. Times like these helped her forgive his indifference and severity, for Percy Witherslack wore his piety heavily, like a coat, and believed everyone should be of like mind. Everyone was a sinner, and his homilies were teeming with the agony of hellfire and punishment for the least of faults or sins. Mary and Emily had no comforts such as the families of other priests of the Church of England; one would think they were Puritans. When she was old enough, Mary was forced to weave cloth and ply her needle so that they could live respectably in others' eyes. What she didn't understand was the depth of his hypocrisy.

When supper was done, she waited as her father fetched his hat and coat and then followed him obediently from the vicarage to St. Edmund Wood, where they were met by Charles Talbot.

"Good afternoon, Mister Witherslack," Talbot greeted with a tip of his hat. He smiled at Mary. "Miss Mary. How pretty you are in the sunlight. Surely Jacob thought the same of Rachel when they met at the well."

"She is not so clever as Rachel," Witherslack sniffed.

"Yet if Jacob saw her as I do now, he would have refused Leah and taken Rachel for his wife on the spot!" chuckled Talbot. He winked at Mary and then turned to Witherslack. "Where are you bound?"

"It is our custom to walk after supper and talk of history and theology. Will you join us?"

"I would be delighted!"

Talbot fell in step with them, and for a while, the stroll was pleasant and silent but for the sounds of nature around them.

"Do you know the ways of the world, Daughter?" Witherslack asked Mary of a sudden.

"Ways?" Mary asked, looking to her father first, and then Charles Talbot, who was smiling at her—not a smile she'd seen before; not a smile one ought to give a fifteen-year-old girl.

"What a stupid child you are!" Witherslack said. "It is simple enough what I ask. Do you know the ways of the world?"

"I wish I knew the 'way' as you mean it, sir."

"The way of men and women together. When they lay abed," Charles Talbot spoke up.

Mary lowered her eyes and felt a hot flush of embarrassment cross her face. "I have heard, and it is a wife's duty to her husband, and a husband to his wife that they are lovers. It is good, and there is sweetness. I have heard these things."

"Is this what Frankewell tells you when he sits too close in church and whispers in your ear?" Witherslack demanded.

"No—!"

"Surely he has suggested it."

"Only of late—" Mary stopped herself in time and shook her head violently.

"He would seduce you and use you as a whore for all manner of sinfulness," Witherslack growled now. "You will not marry such a man! You will not take a papist sympathizer to your bed so that he may corrupt you."

They were in the ruins of the chapter house of the abbey. At any other time, the sunlight pouring through what remained of the windows and the reflections of color from shards of glass that still hung from the frames would have delighted Mary. Still, fear rose up in her throat, and she started to trembled when both men approached slowly, backing her into a column.

"The sinful must atone for their wickedness. And do you know who is wicked?" Witherslack asked.

"The devil is wicked, Father."

Charles Talbot stepped up and roughly took Mary by the throat, sneering at her. "Young girls are wicked, for they entice and lead good Christian men astray, Mary!"

"Do you speak of me, sir?" Mary dared to ask, trying to look at her father, who now had a firm hold on her as if trying to keep her from escaping. "If you do speak of me, I beg of you, please! Let me go. You know that I have always tried to live as godly a life as the Virgin Mary and the saints, as you have taught me…"

"Liar!" Percy Witherslack growled and struck her across the face. "We have seen your flirtations!"

"The men in the village do naught but praise your beauty," Talbot added. "How could they do that, if not by knowledge of it?"

"I have done nothing–!"

"You have seduced that wastrel and rake Erland Frankewell. We have heard his stories when he's been deep in his cups!" Talbot said. "You have uncovered your nakedness here at the abbey and lie with him!

"You'll not marry him! You'll not bed a Papist!" Witherslack hissed as he paced around her. "Wantons must be punished! Whores must be punished!" he murmured huskily as his hands came up around Mary and fondled her breasts.

"Let go of me!"

"Tell us, Mary Witherslack, what is this beauty we hear talk of?" Talbot hissed. "What perfection is it? Show what Erland saw when he stripped you bare and lay with you here out in the open, for all the world to see!"

Talbot ripped open the bodice of her dress, and Mary struggled even more, biting and clawing as her clothes were removed and her father started to undress while he muttered a prayer. Before she lost consciousness, she remembered the tops of the trees and the late afternoon sun shining through them, the silhouette of her father blocking out the sun as he climbed on top of her, and the searing, burning sensation, the horror of what was happening. She saw Abraham Creetur hiding, watching, weeping, and looked to him for help. He fled. When she regained her senses, there was more pain, more of the burning, the bleeding, for Talbot was now taking her by force, panting and coming to climax saying, "'*Your daughters play the whore, and your daughters-in-law commit adultery . . .* '"

Once again, she fell into darkness, but on this occasion, she woke drenched in sweat in the hotel in Canterbury. Could that scream have been hers? A maid was knocking on the door, asking if there was anything wrong.

"It isn't a dream!" Mary whispered to herself and fumbled to get up, tangled in the bedding. She splashed cold water on her face and sat at the dressing table while the knocking continued, and more offers for assistance were made. "Please, I'm just tired, that's all!" Mary called out.

"As long as you're certain, Miss."

"I'm quite sure. Thank you."

A pause and then the soft clip of the maid's boots on the floor as she went away.

Mary had decided to put it behind her to show a happy face when Godwin returned. They would dine in the hotel that evening and take a walk, and he would regale Mary about his interview with the archbishop and how it all worked out to their satisfaction. When Godwin arrived after noon, Mary's resolve failed her, and she began to weep.

"My love! Whatever can be the matter? Mary, darling?" Godwin said when he took her in his arms and then pulled her onto his lap. "All this travel has made you ill. We'll stay in Canterbury for a time,"

"Godwin, I must tell you something," Mary sniffed and hesitantly shared the dream. The words came hesitantly, each after a moment's pause and an episode remembered. Godwin's fierce embrace brought Mary out of the nightmare of memory she'd recounted, and she choked back a sob.

"Hush, Mary! No one will hurt you ever again, I promise!" he vowed.

"I must speak to the archbishop. I will tell him of Charles

Talbot's crimes and my father's."

"Charles Talbot has much to account for. Your father escaped justice,"

"I think not. I believe his fall from a horse wasn't entirely an accident, but no one will listen to me."

After a moment considering this, Godwin nodded. "A carefully placed branch on a road or noise or animal to startle a horse. That happens. My love, do you think Erland—?"

"Who can say? His behavior of the last months would lead one to think . . . I'm sure his parents suspected what happened, and that is why he was sent away."

"They sheltered a murderer?"

"No one in the county can challenge the Frankewells."

"I would. I will uncover their duplicity for all the harm that's been done, especially to you, dearest." Godwin reassured her, holding her close. Mary relaxed in his arms and was happy just to sit within this safe perimeter and listen to the clock ticking and the sounds of an afternoon. When she felt his sigh, she asked, "All went well today?"

"No. It's my word against Talbot's," Godwin answered. "I tried to sound brave and sure just then, didn't I? No one will come forward."

"He would listen to the wife of one of his curates. I'm willing to speak about it now."

"Mary, no, I will not have you shamed further," he protested.

"Nor will I be hidden away in some village or town, every day yet another when I must not think of it, must not speak, and all the while a criminous cleric walks free," countered Mary in a calm, sure voice.

"What about your mother?"

"She should know if she doesn't already. Her reputation is the least of our worries!"

It was decided that they would ask for another interview with the archbishop after the next morning's service. Godwin sent a boy with a message to the cathedral and was relieved when the child returned, although later than anticipated.

"Any news?" Godwin asked, offering the boy a penny and a biscuit.

"He says you are to come at once, sir. He will meet you as soon as you arrive, and I'm to bring you."

Mary reached for her shawl and handed Godwin his hat. She didn't know the message or content of Godwin's letter to the archbishop, but it didn't matter now; it was more than likely the truth.

CHAPTER 17

RAMSAY MAKEPEACE, THE Archbishop of Canterbury, was preparing to return to Lambeth Palace when he learned The Reverend Godwin Herrold requested an audience and had come from Cheshire with the express purpose. Knowing the young man and his history, the Archbishop made the appointment if only to satisfy his curiosity and so postponed the trip to London. He'd not seen Godwin for some time. Had the prodigal son returned? He had indeed, but the interview that morning was disappointing. Godwin offered a list of complaints against the vicar of a poor church on the Welsh Marches, and a few minutes of the diatribe was all Makepeace could stomach. The Bishop of Chester had warned Makepeace about Herrold's business and motives when Herrold approached him not long before he left for Canterbury. Weighing both sides of the dispute, if that is what it was, the Archbishop was skeptical of both men's arguments and was even more concerned when a boy from the hotel arrived that afternoon with an urgent message from Godwin requesting yet another appointment.

Something was not right. Something did not sit well. "Thomas . . ."

Makepeace's secretary looked over his notebook, waiting. The archbishop folded the note from Godwin and handed it over. "Will there be a reply, sir?"

"Send for them now, please. No hesitation."

"Sir. At once."

He moved from his desk to the chair beside the hearth, across from the settle cluttered with vestments and books. What a promising lad, this Godwin Herrold, thought

Makepeace when they first met several years ago. Full of energy, life, passion for his calling. Every day was another opportunity to see God in creation and commune with Him no matter how small or inconsequential the person or problem. That spark of life and youthful joy was missing when he saw Godwin earlier in the day, and it was disconcerting. Perhaps sending Godwin down to placate his father had been the worst of ideas and the most spectacular of failures.

The Bishop of Chester's anxiousness was worrisome. Alfred Morris was a political animal, to be sure, but he seemed overly concerned about whatever it was that Godwin was trying to bring out to the open. Makepeace regretted having cut off the boy before he had a chance to plead his case. Well, he'd have another chance soon enough.

From a cassock pocket, Makepeace took Morris' letter and unfolded it with the same care he used to fold Godwin's. For the second time that day, he carefully and slowly read the handwriting that was jagged and sloppy from palsy, like strands of yarn tangled on the floor.

> *'Your Excellency:*
>
> *We greet you well.*
>
> *It has come to my attention, Your Grace, that one of my priests resigned his curacy at Saint Ælfgiva's Knowstone here in Cheshire. This was done without my knowledge or consent, and I seek inquiry as to the true purpose of this sudden departure. What I do know is that the young man is an intimate acquaintance of yours, a young man from the Weald whose father is a member of the House of Commons and sits for Crowborough. Of course, it is Godwin Herrold of whom I write, a secretary in your lordship's household until he arrived in Cheshire.*
>
> *It is my understanding that he is set for Canterbury with the sole purpose of seeking an audience with you to share a wild tale of criminous clerics in Knowstone. Knowstone, of all places! It is a*

village in the middle of nothing. I urge you, sir, to consider the bearer of this tale. It is said he still grieves for his murdered wife, and he spends most of his day sitting in the corner of a public house listening to tittle-tattle or keeping company with the questionable young men of the shire. I know that he has quarreled openly with the new vicar, The Reverend Charles Talbot, who succeeded the late vicar, Percy Witherslack, an unfortunate man who died in a hunting accident in Saint Edmund Wood. Godwin Herrold has an ax to grind and will not be content until he has ruined Mister Talbot, and that would be unfortunate for all of Knowstone and those in Cheshire who know Talbot's Godly worth. Such eloquence! Such piety! It is not to be believed that a humble man like Talbot could be guilty of anything save modesty.

> *'Yours in Christ and Faithfully I remain,*
> *+ Alfred Chester.'*

If Godwin was anything, he was not vindictive nor jealous of another man's fortune or rise. It sounded as if Morris, in his last sentences, was describing Godwin for all of his virtues.

No, something was not right.

"Mister Herrold and his wife, Your Grace."

"Thank you, Thomas. Show them in."

Back at the desk, Makepeace put aside the sermon he'd been writing and stacked Bibles on top of commentaries on the desk end, using the task to formulate counter-arguments to whatever young Herrold might have brought back with him. He was prepared to set a stern countenance and be all business when the couple entered. His eyes went immediately to the beautiful young woman on Godwin's arm, and Makepeace knew he was gaping by the way Godwin looked at his wife and then at him, smiling. Gone were the morose and defeated looks from that morning. This young man looked quite contented, and it was easy to tell why.

"Your Grace, may I present my bride, Mary Burnley, now

Herrold, daughter of The Reverend Percy Witherslack," Godwin introduced after greetings were exchanged and tea was set before them.

"Witherslack. I am not acquainted with any cleric by that name," Makepeace confessed.

"My father was called from London to Cheshire, Your Grace. Cheshire is a long way from Canterbury," replied Mary.

"It is, and you have absolved me of my ignorance with that observation, my dear! I'm sorry to confess that I will be near to death by the time I've traveled to the ends of England learn the names and faces of every one of my clergy," Makepeace chuckled. He sobered just as quickly and gestured toward the refreshments. "Well, let us have cups of tea all around, and then you must tell me what's so grave and urgent that you should want to see me twice in one day," Makepeace opened. "Am I to understand this concerns you, Mistress Herrold?"

"It does, sir, but I beg you to forgive me for not speaking out sooner," Mary answered. "You see, Archbishop, I have been wronged, and it is time I receive satisfaction."

"Yes. Indeed?" the tone was skeptical, the words drawn out.

"It is no folly or silly hurt, Your Grace, I do assure you."

Fashionably attired, a trim and fetching figure with high breasts and by her height and the way her muslin skirts draped her torso, long shapely legs, the perfectly proportioned oval face, and large blue eyes—where had Godwin found this goddess of good society and family? Makepeace doubted she'd been wronged in the least; this girl looked as if she was accustomed to getting what she wanted and made those who did not grant her wishes suffer for their indifference or refusal. He'd put an end to this straight away.

"Your good name blackened by a harsh word from the pulpit? A compliment mistook for adulterous flirtation?" Makepeace said in jest, winking.

"Nothing as foolish, sir."

"I'm surprised you say that Mistress Herrold, for one such as you, I'm sure would find insult in the smallest attempt to secure your attention or affection. Men are fools, you know. Do you think a young woman's reputation can be sullied by the foolish words of old men in their fumbling to flatter someone as beautiful as you?" Makepeace asked, trying not to smile.

"The crimes are more serious. I beg your leave to say them. Otherwise, I know not what else to do except speak with the constabulary in Cheshire."

Makepeace cleared his throat and then tried to hold back a chuckle. The nerve of this chit of a girl used to getting her way because she was made to believe she too beautiful to turn down!

"I see that you mock me, sir, and doubt the seriousness of my complaint."

Mary rose to leave but was stayed by Makepeace's hand on her arm. If ever a woman's glance could change a man's mind, it was at that moment when Makepeace looked up at the young woman and saw the anger and seriousness, the hurt.

After a moment, Makepeace nodded. "Continue, Mistress Herrold."

"I wish to bring charges against The Reverend Mister Talbot. Not only in the ecclesiastical court but the secular courts of law." Mary paused to catch her breath and was given the courage to continue by the silence and look of concern from Makepeace. "It comes to this: Mister Talbot and my father used me in ways . . . that is, they took advantage of my youth and innocence . . . they raped me several times from the age of fifteen until I ran away with my late husband when I was not yet twenty."

"Can this be true?" Makepeace gasped.

"Why should my wife lie, Your Grace?" Godwin asked.

"Why did you not come forward when the crime was first committed?" Makepeace now demanded. "Why did you allow this to happen?"

"The word of a fifteen-year-old girl already treated with

suspicion by villagers because of her interest in education and a lack of conformity to the rules of society would be ignored, and yet another cause for disdain. I am not Dinah and have no brothers to champion me."

Her reference to a biblical heroine and an obscure one at that gave Makepeace pause.

"And your mother, I assume, encouraged you to come to me?"

"I do not doubt she was a party to it or knew about it and kept her silence."

"To protect your life and hers, I think? Your reputations?"

Mary frowned and said after a moment, "That would be the best-kept secret, Your Grace. She wanted me gone from that time, and when I did return after my husband's death, she made it clear I was unwanted and unloved. I was a burden."

Makepeace rose and took a tour of the room, hands behind back and head down as he walked slowly, purposefully, as if he was in a museum gallery viewing a collection, for he paused before each painting, artifact, and icon, noted something about them in particular, and then continued. He stopped at the hearth and suddenly turned on Mary. "I pray this is not a misguided cry for a mother's love or attention—"

"God's life!" Mary was on her feet and clenching her fists at her side. When Godwin shifted to calm her, she batted him away. "Do you think I endured the pain, the humiliation, the physical torment for my mother's love? To beg her to pay attention to me?" she cried. "Shall I show you the scars on my body? Shall I take you to the grave of the child? If it were possible, I would show you the scars on my heart and soul! Good day, Archbishop! I will take my complaint elsewhere."

"Mary!" Godwin leaped to prevent her from leaving the room, and Makepeace noted how she steeled herself against her husband's gentle touch. Looking at her, Makepeace did not doubt she spoke truly. The sadness in her eyes, the way she trembled yet held her head high and met his gaze, and such independence! Not once did she look at her husband for prompting or reassurance. Mary's deportment and the hesitant, humble delivery of this message, the blushes that rose in her cheeks were proof of her seriousness. Her story told, the emotion was too much even for such a strong young woman. Tears now spilled onto her face, and she looked away to dab at them with a handkerchief, turning back again when she was more composed.

"This is, in addition to the abuses and crimes I tried to speak of before," Godwin added quietly, "but you dismissed them as envy for Talbot's place and living."

Makepeace was ready to chide Godwin for his impertinence but thought better of it. He sighed, then, saying, "That I did and more the fault's mine. But Godwin, Mary, these are serious accusations."

"They are the truth, Your Grace," Godwin answered. "Mary and I can tell you of eight families in Bottle Street in Knowstone who have suffered at his hands."

"And those of my father," Mary added.

"Do you know of Charnel House School in Wattling?" Godwin asked Makepeace.

"No, I can't say that I have. And is that a name of a school? Horrible!"

"What was done to boys who did not behave or for the fault of their parents who could not pay tuition is the horror. Charles Talbot is the trustee of this school and sees to its daily running. Such things that may not be spoken of—depravity, sexual slavery, and corporal punishment that led to death for some. . ."

Makepeace held up his hand for silence and said quietly, "Enough, please. Enough. Be certain. Be very certain that you understand what you allege here and how it will affect all concerned. The loss of reputation, the loss of income, vocation, indeed, criminal charges, for the constabulary will need to be informed of this and make an investigation. Mistress Herrold, you will be a figure of slander and lost to good society. These are serious charges."

"Has that not already happened? Yet I survived. I wish to face my tormentor and see that justice is done," Mary answered.

"You are a remarkable young woman," Makepeace said. He went back to his desk and sat, took a quill, and started to write, saying, "Have you leave to stay in Canterbury? I would like to take statements from both of you in the presence of a solicitor and a canon lawyer. I will not proceed with letters dimissory nor release the accused to a criminal trial without evidence or a fair hearing. You bear the burden of proof, and it will not be easy."

"I am not afraid, sir, for God is with me."

Godwin was taken aback by Mary's comment. She, who had little cause to trust in the Lord for all the misfortune in her life . . .

"You will go to the Bishop of Chester with a letter I shall give you. It will be my consent for an inquiry to proceed immediately."

"Thank you, sir. Your Grace," Godwin stammered, "we'll say good afternoon, then."

"We'll meet tomorrow at three o'clock."

"Certainly, and thank you again."

The Archbishop's secretary appeared and showed them out, Makepeace listening as the footsteps faded and a door closed. He looked up when Thomas reentered, notebook and pencil in hand. "Shall I make the arrangements for tomorrow?" he queried.

Makepeace leaned his chin on folded hands and considered the question. "Give me time to think about that. Herrold and his wife have nowhere to go. They'll stay in Canterbury as long as they have hope. I'll give them an answer."

Nodding, Thomas went back to his desk in the outer office. He was seated and ready to see what the next order of business was when he heard the laughter and glanced out the window.

Godwin and Mary Herrold were walking through the cloister to the street, arm in arm, until he swung his wife up in his arms and kissed her. If it were Thomas making the decision, he already knew in whose favor it would be.

CHAPTER 18

EMILY OPENED HER eyes and glared at Cook, standing over her and smelling disagreeably of lamb stew and soap. The combined aromas rather than the strange gentleman in her parlor woke her up from a nap.

"Did I tell not you there'll be no interruptions nor callers? You know that I'm not well! How shall I mend with these constant interruptions hour after hour?" whined Emily as she threw off the shawl and sat upright on the settee. She ignored Cook and looked directly at the gentleman. "Who are you?" she demanded. "What's your business?"

"This is a constable from Chester, M'am," Cook started.

"Chester! What business do you have in Knowstone? Ah! Is it my daughter? Have you found her? Is she dead?"

Emily's questions weren't fraught with anxiety or fear. Each of them was a demand void of emotion. This lack of concern would have been curious to the unfamiliar, if not suspicious, but to Cook and others in Knowstone, it was an appropriate response for Emily Witherslack.

The constable stepped forward as he removed his hat and nodded in greeting. "Your daughter is well and is living in Cambridge with her husband, M'am. I have come on a matter brought before the constabulary by the Bishop of Chester and the Archbishop of Canterbury," he explained.

"Let me guess. She married the priest, didn't she?" Emily hissed at Cook, who merely shrugged. Emily's eyes narrowed. "Chester and Canterbury, you say? What has Mister Herrold done?" she now demanded of the constable.

"Your pardon, Mistress Witherslack, but he's done well for himself and his wife from what I know, and that isn't much, as that is not my concern. My business today is with you. There is a complaint Mistress Herrold has brought to our attention, and it has to do with her late father, who I assume is your late husband."

"Let the dead rest in peace, sir! The child never loved her father or me for that matter! She had not one thimble full of respect nor regard. The way she eloped with that rakish professor and left her fiancé, a man of good parentage and society, broken-hearted so that he took his life from the shame of her rejection! And then to come back here and play the distraught widow and victim! It's been almost a year to the day that she ran off to God knows where to live in sin with that miserable priest! Take your concern elsewhere. I've no mind to speak with you of my poor, late husband, especially since I've tried so hard to forget!"

The Constable shrugged. "That's not what I heard. If you haven't any time, Mistress Witherslack, I'll say good afternoon, but you will oblige me another day? I'm expected at Saltfield."

"What? Why would you go there?" Emily asked.

"I spoke with Lady Isobel this morning, and now I'm going to speak with her maid. The young lady wants to retract a nasty story she told about your daughter and to discuss other matters. I warrant that the little maid's memory is as good as Lady Isobel's insofar as your daughter is concerned. Good day."

Emily went white as a sheet.

℘

THE CONSTABLE'S REPORT arrived by post to Cambridge a week later, brought to a tidy little shop in the high street where the proprietress and her husband lived on the second and third floors. Mary studied the letter handed to her and then turned the sign about on the door, going upstairs. Godwin was in the small sitting room with the rector of St. Bene't's Church, The Reverend Mister Poperly, when Mary appeared in the doorway.

"Godwin, dearest,"

"Mary? Is something the matter?"

Godwin and the rector were on their feet as she approached, holding the letter out.

"This is from the Chester Constabulary. It arrived just now."

Poperly offered to leave, but Godwin bade him stay to witness whatever news the letter held, good or bad. Godwin opened the letter and studied it for a moment. Sighing, he said, "Your mother won't cooperate, and neither will the Bishop of Chester despite the Archbishop's request. They dismiss your claims as girlish hysteria."

"He has no choice but to obey the Archbishop," Poperly sniffed.

"What does this mean? Will Talbot not answer for his crimes?" Mary wanted to know.

"He will, but it shall take longer than we wished," Godwin replied. "I'll send word to the Archbishop, although he assuredly knows what they're doing in Knowstone and will act upon it!"

"I have no doubt of it, Godwin," Poperly said. "You have my support in this, and I hope, when autumn comes, you will accept the Vestry's proposal and answer the call to Saint Bene't's Cambridge."

"Godwin!" Mary squealed with delight. She threw herself into his arms for a kiss. "Why did you never say a word?"

"Weightier matters cloud my mind, sweetheart, but I was going to surprise you on our wedding anniversary."

"Shall you be the curate?" Mary asked.

"The rector."

Mary looked to Poperly, who said, "I am retiring and looking to spend time in the Lake District. We know St. Bene't's will be in good hands. On your holidays you will come to stay with me. What do you say?"

"I've never known such happiness!" said Mary as she hugged Godwin again.

That happiness was with them when they rode back to the west of England and the Welsh marches some months later.

Knowstone enjoyed the scandal caused by Mary Burnley and Godwin Herrold's departures, their names bandied around The Castle and Motte, neighbors leaning on gates and saying, "I told you so!" Homilies preached every Sunday warning of the sins of the flesh. The titillation was stale and boring by a month mind, and soon the lovers were but distant memories. Life in Knowstone got on; the market held on Saturday, and the lamps lit at dusk. The good wives assembled in front of the church on Sundays after Morning Prayer or Holy Eucharist and shared gossip. Even the tragic end of Erland Frankewell was forgotten as the Frankewell family prepared for Jane's wedding to Robert Marchmont. No one gave a second thought to the young cleric and his wife when they arrived in Knowstone, for it was assumed they were guests for the wedding.

At Hazelwick, Cook heard the jangle of the rusting bell and wiped her hands upon her already greasy apron, ready to upbraid the fool that had come to call so early in the day. The pies would be ruined if she didn't get back to them.

"You look like you've seen a ghost," Mary teased. "Do close your mouth, dearest Meg—you're bound to catch flies!"

"Mistress Burnley! Mary! Is it you? Look at you!" Cook exclaimed.

"Cook!" Emily shouted from the top of the stairs. "I smell something burning!"

"Straight away, M'am. But do come down! You have a visitor!" Cook shouted back.

"How many times have I ordered you not to shout? Another shilling from your wage packet, my girl!"

"Do come down, Mistress!"

Emily nearly swooned at the sight of her daughter standing in the middle of the parlor. She was radiant in a becoming apricot frock and *pelisse*, the same as that which graced the dress shop window a year ago. As they offered sterile kisses in greeting, Emily noted the wedding ring on the girl's left hand and said, "So it's true. You are a married woman again and not a model for degenerate and reprobate artists, nor living in sin with your lover."

"We were properly married in a church, Emily," Godwin replied as he entered. He avoided the way Emily raked her eyes over him and her attention flickering from Mary to him, how she softened and tapped his arm coquettishly.

"Mister Talbot will be relieved to hear it, for no doubt you've come to resume your curacy and just in time! He is nearly dead for all that he must do, and tomorrow is the wedding, the most important wedding all year! Jane Frankewell is to marry Robert Marchmont! And Mary, do you know she will wear the dress you made for her!"

"I have a message from the bishop to Mister Talbot, and I have come on the authority of the Archbishop, Mistress Witherslack, to relieve Mister Talbot of his duties here," Godwin answered.

"Are you then to be rector?" she wanted to know, forcing a smile.

"No. We are on our way from Chester back to Cambridge." Godwin paused as Cook entered with a tray of sandwiches and lemonade.

"Come, sit down, and we'll take refreshment," Emily offered. "You may tell me all about your wedding."

Godwin waited for Mary to sit and then took his place beside her, Emily noting with bitterness and envy how he refused to let go of her hand or remove his eyes from her. If they were bent on staying the night, she'd give them the north rooms where she wouldn't have to hear their lovemaking, for it was apparent after a year that that fire had not yet died and looked as if it never would.

"We were married at Saint Bene't's Church Cambridge," Mary replied simply. "A small wedding supper. Godwin has been called as rector to Saint Bene't's."

"Is he? Tell me, Mister Herrold, Godwin, if not you for vicar here in Knowstone, then why is Mister Talbot soon to be redundant?" Emily wanted to know, handing him a second sandwich.

"The Archbishop has been considering this action for some time. You need not worry."

"And why should I not be concerned? Mister Talbot is our priest. I'm sure the good people of Knowstone would have something to say about it!"

"Why should the Archbishop listen to them when for so many years they shut their eyes and ears to things which may not be spoken of?" asked Godwin.

"You're being vague purposefully, sir! Come! Say what it is and stop playing games," Emily snapped.

"Charles Talbot is called to answer charges of rape and adultery," Godwin replied matter-of-factly, taking a third sandwich.

"Rape and adultery—? Surely the Archbishop is mistaken, for Charles Talbot is a sober man," Emily replied, tittering nervously.

"Is he?" Mary asked.

"I would I knew his accuser or accusers!" Emily declared passionately. "I will be glad to speak for him!"

"Will you?" Mary demanded quietly. She raised her brows at Emily, who looked away and fussed with the shawl draped around her shoulders, complaining of a sudden chill, her weariness.

"You ought to reconsider your valiant offer," Godwin said. Your late husband was fortunate to have met with a foul accident to prevent this same embarrassment to you."

Emily felt a cold sweat over her entire body and avoided Mary's gaze. "Will you defame a man not so long in his grave?" she hissed.

"The grave is best for him. The world is better off," Mary said.

Emily finally looked at the girl and said nothing but began to weep. "What I have had to endure! Women are born to bear heavy burdens and be thankful for their lot! What could I have done? Who would have believed me? I beg of you, Mary, I beg of you—!"

"Yet you shamed me and despised me for what they did!" Mary replied.

"I fear we've upset Mistress Witherslack, my love. Let's go back to the inn." Godwin suggested and rose, taking Mary by the hand.

"You will not stay?" Emily asked, suddenly calm, her tears wiped away. "I can ask Mister Bede and Mistress Galthwaite to dine with us. It will be a lovely party. Surely you will not go elsewhere? It will be said…"

"It will be said that Mistress Herrold goes where she is welcome."

Godwin and Mary left, Emily's protests dissolving into new tears.

The next morning when Godwin and Mary entered the church, three ladies of the altar guild were decorating the nave for the wedding that afternoon: white lilies and tulips, freesia, carnations were everywhere, festooned with white ribbons. Mary's gasped in surprise to find her fair linen gracing the altar in the sanctuary. Godwin noted it too, also taking a count of the frowns and stares of the women. His business here wouldn't take long; he had no desire to make his wife miserable. He brought Mary to the sanctuary steps, kissed her gently, and bade her wait while he went to find Talbot. Talbot entered from the porch as Godwin was climbing the steps to the sacristy. He turned when he heard his name shouted.

"It's true, then! You dare to return, you stupid fool!" Talbot hissed, mindless of the activity around them. "I should have you run out of Knowstone on a rail, or better, tarred and feathered! Leave at once! Both of you!"

"You're strangely truculent and angry where it concerns others' sins, Talbot," Godwin remarked, stepping forward. He reached into the pocket of his topcoat and took out a document heavy with seals. "Here is a letter from Ramsay, Archbishop of Canterbury."

"Let me guess, by some artifice or invention, you've managed to become his secretary again! God forbid you should earn anything by merit alone!" Talbot now spat and tore open the letter. "It confounds the soul to cipher how a fool like you would come into his confidence. . ."

Suddenly, he made guttural sounds as if being strangled, and the document dropped from his hands, falling into the path of a woman placing candles on the altar. She stooped to retrieve it, but Talbot managed to recover and snatched it away to read the letter again.

"I trust you understand the charges against you?" Godwin queried in a voice no one but Talbot could hear. He continued, saying, "What you have in your hands is your death warrant, or something like it, Talbot. Did you not think you'd have to pay eventually for your sins? It is a dear price, I fear!" Godwin then motioned to a gentleman waiting in the shadows, who came forward and introduced himself as a constable of Cheshire.

While Talbot trembled in fury and tried hard to control his temper, Godwin led Mary from the church. Later that afternoon, when all of Knowstone was celebrating Jane Frankewell's marriage, they boarded a coach, which trundled off as soon as they were settled and the doors slammed shut. In the darkness of the swaying cabin, Godwin touched Mary's face tenderly.

"Did I not say it would be easy, Darling Mary?" he whispered.

"Let's be gone. I will not be content until we are through the wood and returned to Cambridge," she sighed.

"Our home," Godwin echoed, wrapping her in his arms. He rested her head on his shoulder and kept her in his safe and loving embrace as the London coach trundled up and down through the narrow streets of Knowstone, past the ruined abbey and to the observer, nothing more than a firefly speck of light in the darkness of St. Edmund Wood.

Here Endeth the Lesson

About the Author

ELLEN L. EKSTROM is a native of the San Francisco Bay Area. Educated locally, she holds a bachelor's degree in theological studies, concentrating on historical theology. She prefers to write historical and fantasy fiction, although she is known to take detours into matters concerning the modern heart. To discover more about Ellen and Whyte Rose & Violet Scribes' growing catalog of titles, please visit:
www.whyteroseandviolet.net.

Also by Ellen L. Ekstrom

The Legacy
Armor of Light
Ascalon
Tallis' Third Tune
(Midwinter Sonata, Book 1)
Scarborough – Quinn's Story
(Midwinter Sonata, Book 2)
The Shop Girl of Flowergate
What She Wished For . . .A Cautionary Tale